Hurrah for the Circus!

By Enid Blyton

HINKLER BOOKS

Cover Illustration: Gilly Marklew, sga Illustration & Design, UK
Illustrations: Gilly Marklew, sga Illustration & Design, UK
Typesetting: Palmer Higgs, Box Hill, Victoria, Australia

Hurrah for the Circus!
First published in 1939 by George Newnes
This edition published in 2004 by Hinkler Books Pty Ltd
17–23 Redwood Drive
Dingley VIC 3172 Australia
www.hinklerbooks.com

ISBN 1 7412 1431 9
Printed and bound in Australia

The Author
Enid Blyton

Enid Blyton is one of the best-loved writers of the twentieth century. Her wonderful, inventive stories, plays and poems have delighted children of all ages for generations.

Born in London in 1897, Enid Blyton sold her first piece of literature; a poem entitled 'Have You …?' at the age of twenty. She qualified and worked as a teacher, writing extensively in her spare time. She sold short stories and poems to various magazines and her first book, *Child Whispers*, was published in 1922.

Over the next 40 years, Blyton would publish on average fifteen books a year. Some of her more famous works include *Noddy*, *The Famous Five*, *The Secret Seven* and *The Faraway Tree* series.

Her books have sold in the millions and have been translated into many languages. Enid Blyton married twice and had two daughters. She died in 1968, but her work continues to live on.

Contents

Oh, here comes the circus!

Mr Galliano Again

Tan-tan-tara! Tan-tan-tara! Tan-tan-tan-tan-tan-tara!

The noise of trumpets came down the main street of the town, and all the children rushed out of their houses, and the grown-ups went to their windows.

'What is it? What is it? It's the circus coming! Listen to the trumpets! Oh, look, here come the first lovely black horses! Oh, here comes the circus! Hurrah for the circus!'

Come along out with all the children and watch the circus coming through the town. Whose circus is it? It is Mr Galliano's famous circus—and look, there is his beautiful carriage, glittering like gold! Do you see Mr Galliano sitting in it, handsome and strong, with his enormous black moustaches curling upwards?

He takes off his top hat and bows to us! His black-haired wife smiles too, and waves her plump hand. After the glittering carriage comes a string of beautiful white horses, shining like silk, their proud heads tossing in the air!

'*Up* there, *up* there!' cries pretty Pepita, who is riding the first one, and her horse walks a few steps on his hind legs, whilst all the watching children cheer loudly. Behind Pepita come her sister and brother, Juanita and Lou, riding their horses grandly, bowing to everyone they pass. Then comes old Sticky Stanley the clown, in his comic suit of red and black, blowing a trumpet and banging a kettle for a drum, and throwing sweets to the children.

'Come and watch me at the circus!' cried Stanley. 'I'm the best bit of the circus, I am!' And then he put the kettle on the top of his head and danced so comically that all the children ran alongside to watch him.

Now come the caravans, the bright houses on wheels, and how the children wish they could peep inside and see the circus folk cooking their dinners! What fun it must be to live in a caravan.

Now look at this glorious yellow caravan with bright curtains fluttering in the wind. Do you know who it belongs to? Of course you do! It belongs to Jimmy, our old friend Jimmy, who lives there with his mother and father and Lotta. Lotta's parents are away for six months with their horses, so Lotta is living with Mr and Mrs Brown, Jimmy's mother and father.

There she is, peeping out of the caravan, her black curls dancing. And there is Jimmy, sitting on the steps at the back, and on his knee lies Lucky, his famous dog!

We get a wag from Lucky, that clever little fox-terrier, who is as smart as paint. Lucky can walk the tight-rope, she can count, and she can spell! Oh, Lucky is a marvellous dog, and Jimmy loves her with all his heart and is very proud of her.

That is Mr Brown driving the caravan. Beside him sits a plump black spaniel, Lulu, a faithful dog that Jimmy and Lotta once saved from two cruel people. She is not clever, but she is very loving and a splendid watch-dog. Do you see Mrs Brown in the caravan? She is cooking the dinner—and a good one it is, if we can judge by the smell!

Now what a shout goes up! Here is the elephant! Jumbo plods by, flapping his ears, and holding out his trunk for a bun. Let's give him one! He pops it into his big mouth at once, and Mr Tonks, his keeper, nods a 'thank you' to us. He is a kind little man, who loves his elephant better than anything else in the world.

Jumbo is strong. He pulls three cages behind him. In one is Sammy, the famous chimpanzee, and today he wears an old hat belonging to Mrs Brown, and is very proud of it. Funny old Sammy!

'What can your chimpanzee do?' yell the watching children to Mr Wally, his keeper.

'All the things that *you* can!' yells back Mr Wally. 'He can dress and undress himself—put himself to bed—ride a bicycle—clean his teeth—brush his hair! You come and watch him tomorrow night!'

Sammy puts his hat on back to front and waves to the children, smiling in his chimpanzee way. He is wishing that little dog Lucky would come and play with him, for he loves Lucky.

There is another cage behind Sammy's, and in it we see the three clever monkeys belonging to Lilliput, the little man sitting on the step. They are all dressed in red woollen coats, for the weather is still cold. They cuddle one another, and chatter to the watching children. Lilliput has his fourth monkey with him, little Jemima. She lies round his neck like a fur, whispering into his ear, and sometimes nibbling Lilliput's red hair! Funny little Jemima, she is full of tricks, and everyone loves her, though she can be very mischievous indeed when she likes!

With shouting, clapping, and cheering the circus goes by to the field where it is to camp. What a busy time it is when the circus folk set up their tents! How they shout and hunt for things they have dropped, and how quickly they settle in for a few days, making a camp of the big field, doing their washing,

4

cooking their meals, practising their clever turns in the big red ring!

And now let us go to see our old friends, Jimmy and Lotta. We shall find them by the yellow caravan. Mrs Brown is calling them to come and eat. Mr Brown, who is odd-job man in the circus, has gone off to help with the tents, munching sandwiches as he goes. He is the busiest man there at these times, for everyone wants him at once! 'Brownie!' they call, 'Brownie! Give me a hand here! Brownie, where are you?'

And Mr Brown rushes from one to another with his tools, putting everything right.

It is Easter-time. The circus is at Westsea, and the field they are camping in is quite near the sea. Jimmy and Lotta listened to the noise of the waves as they ate their sausages, and held their hot potatoes, cooked in their skins.

'I've never been to the sea before!' said Jimmy. 'Oh, Lotta, what fun we'll have here! We'll go walking on the sands every day before breakfast!'

'Wuff!' said Lucky, licking Jimmy's hand.

'Yes, you shall come too,' said Jimmy, patting the little dog on her soft head. 'And so shall Lulu. Mother, have you got a sausage for Lulu? She's hungry. Lucky has had a good meal. She mustn't have any more.'

Mrs Brown threw a sausage to Lulu—but before the spaniel could get it, a little brown creature flashed out from under the caravan and snatched it up. In a trice she was away across the field, with Lulu after her.

'It's Jemima, the bad monkey!' cried Jimmy. 'Chase her, Lulu! Get your sausage!'

The two children laughed as they watched plump Lulu run after the artful monkey. Jemima did not want the sausage for herself, for she did not like sausages—but she did love teasing poor Lulu! When Lulu had run three times round the field after her, the little monkey ran up to the top of Jimmy's caravan and put the sausage on the edge of the roof, where Lulu could see and smell it but couldn't reach it!

'Jemima, you want a scolding!' laughed Jimmy. Mrs Brown took a stick and knocked down the sausage. Lulu was quick enough at getting it this time! Two bites and a swallow and that sausage was gone! Jemima made the funny little chattering noise that was her laugh, and scampered away to Lilliput's caravan. He was looking for her, a juicy orange in his hand. She was the only one of his four monkeys that was allowed out loose, for she was as tame as a child.

Jimmy and Lotta finished their meal, and then they went to give a hand where they could. Jimmy offered to take old Jumbo down to the stream to drink water and wash himself, whilst Mr Tonks finished putting up the big elephant's tent.

'Right you are, Jimmy,' said Mr Tonks, who knew that the little boy could be trusted with any animal in the world. 'Up, Jumbo!'

Jumbo curled his trunk gently round Jimmy and set him high up on his big broad neck. Then he set off for the stream that ran like a shining thread in the next field.

Lotta went to help Pepita and Juanita with their beautiful white horses. There was plenty of work to do with their string of sleek, shining animals, and the little girl adored every one of them, and took a great deal of trouble to keep them healthy, well-fed, and silky.

She no longer rode in the ring as she used to do when her mother and father, Lal and Laddo, kept their horses in the circus. Lal and Laddo were far away in a strange land, where they had taken their own beautiful horses and their clever dogs. Lotta missed them, and longed for the time for them to come back, when she might once more ride in the ring on her own horse.

But Jimmy went into the ring every night with little dog Lucky—and how the people cheered him when they saw the boy running into the ring, dressed in his wonderful suit that glittered like silver fire! He swung his red velvet cloak, and bowed proudly to the cheering people.

'Good old Jimmy! Good old Lucky!' shouted everyone. 'Show us what you can do!'

Fun for Jimmy and Lotta

It was lovely by the sea at Easter-time. Behind the circus camp rose the green hills, blazing with golden gorse.

'It smells like warm coconut,' said Lotta, sniffing. 'Isn't it lovely! I wish I could eat it!'

'You might as well eat a hedgehog!' laughed Jimmy. 'I'd like to wear a bit of gorse for a button-hole, but it's too prickly to pick.'

Bluebells were beginning to grow in the sheltered patches here and there. Pale primroses peeped in the damp spots, and Jimmy and Lotta picked a great bunch to take back to the caravan. They were very happy.

Sometimes they walked on the hills with Lucky and Lulu, sometimes they walked by the sea, if the tide was out. They took off their shoes then, and splashed in the little waves. Lucky ran after the white edges of the waves as they came up on the sands and ran down again. She picked up a long strand of ribbon-like seaweed and tore down the beach with it streaming behind her.

'Quite mad!' said Lotta. 'Look—now she's got her nose in a pool! Whatever has she found there?'

It was a crab, very angry at being disturbed. Lucky pawed the water to try and get it, and the crab began to bury itself in the wet sand. Lucky nosed it out—and then she gave a loud bark of fright and shot backwards about ten feet, her tail down. She scraped hard at her nose.

Lotta gave a squeal of laughter. 'The crab's pinched her nose, Jimmy!'

'Poor old Lucky!' said Jimmy. 'Don't interfere with crabs, and they won't interfere with you!'

'I do miss all the dogs we used to have!' sighed Lotta, kicking a stone along the beach. 'I wish Lal and Laddo had left them for me to look after. I could have gone into the ring with them then. As it is, I don't go any more. I feel quite jealous of you, Jimmy, going in every night, and getting such loud cheers and claps!'

'Don't be jealous, Lotta,' said Jimmy. 'Why, you have belonged to the circus ever since you were born. I only came last year! You're a long way ahead of me, really. Perhaps Juanita, Pepita and Lou will let you work with them soon. They might let you have one of their horses for your own, and you could ride that.'

'I'll ask them when we get back,' said Lotta, cheering up. 'Let's go back now. Lulu! Lucky! Home!'

Lulu came racing out of the water, shaking her silky spaniel coat. Lucky tore up, carrying a piece of seaweed which she dropped at Jimmy's feet.

Jimmy stuck the seaweed on to a stick and gave it to Lucky. 'Up then, Lucky!' he said. 'This is a flag now, and you are a captain, carrying it. Up!'

Up went Lucky on her hind legs, the stick stuck in the crook of a front leg. She strutted along behind the two children with little steps, her tail wagging hard. Lulu looked at her solemnly. She thought Lucky was most extraordinary when she began to do tricks. Lulu couldn't even beg!

Lucky showed off in front of Lulu. She put up her head and strutted along proudly—and splash she went into a pool of water that she didn't see!

The children laughed, and began to run. 'We'd better hurry home now the dogs are wet,' panted Jimmy. 'We must dry them well, for the wind is cold even though the sun is warm!'

The two dogs had a good rub down. Jimmy was always very careful with any animal under his care, and he knew at once if any of them were out of sorts or unhappy.

'Look! There's old Jumbo bathing in the sea!' cried Lotta, pointing. And sure enough, there was Jumbo solemnly wading into the water, filling his trunk and squirting it over himself. He saw the children and his little eyes shone.

'Hello, Jumbo!' cried Lotta, and she danced near him. Quickly the elephant pointed his trunk towards her and tried to soak her with the water he had drawn up. But Lotta was up to old Jumbo's tricks and she ran away, laughing.

Back at the camp the children were set to work.

'Lotta, fetch me some water from the stream,' called Mrs Brown. 'And, Jimmy, Mr Wally wants you to help him to clean out Sammy's cage.'

'Right,' said Jimmy. 'I'll just rub down these two dogs first!'

He got their towels and rubbed them dry. Lulu licked his hand and went to lie down on the mat inside the caravan. Lucky, like a little shadow, followed at Jimmy's heels when he went across the field to Mr Wally's smart caravan and the cage where Sammy the chimpanzee lived in comfort.

But the cage was empty! Jimmy looked round. Where was Mr Wally, and where was the chimpanzee? The cage door was open and the cage was half washed out.

'Look! There's old Jumbo bathing in the sea.'

'Mr Wally! Where are you? Do you want me to help you?' shouted Jimmy.

A scared face looked out from under Mr Wally's caravan. It was one of the grooms, a man kept to help with Mr Galliano's marvellous black horses.

'Is Mr Wally about?' he asked, in a whisper.

'I can't see him,' said Jimmy, puzzled. 'What are you hiding for?'

The man crept out and shook himself. 'I said I'd help Mr Wally clean the cage,' he said. 'And I left the door unlatched. Well, that wretched chimpanzee slipped out behind my back, threw a scrubbing-brush at me, and disappeared! Mr Wally came along, and he was so angry when he saw the cage empty that I hid under here.'

'But where's Sammy?' asked Jimmy, alarmed.

'How should I know?' said the man sulkily. 'I'm engaged to help with the horses, I am, and I'm not going to have anything more to do with chimps.'

He went off, muttering. Jimmy caught sight of Mr Wally at the other side of the field, and he ran across to him.

'Have you got Sammy?' he called.

'No,' said Mr Wally, looking worried. 'That silly fellow must have frightened him, and he's disappeared. He'll come back all right, but I don't want any harm to come to him. Hunt around a bit, Jimmy, and call him.'

So the two of them hunted about the caravans and tents, calling to Sammy—but there wasn't a sign of him anywhere! Lucky snifffed about too, but all she did was to keep running to Jimmy's own caravan and back to Jimmy, so that wasn't much help! Jimmy's caravan was shut, for his mother had gone shopping and his father was busy. There was no one there. Lotta had not yet come back with the water.

Mrs Brown came back very soon, carrying a basket full of eggs and butter. She was surprised to see Jimmy and Wally and Lotta looking so upset, and hunting everywhere for Sammy. She went up the steps of her caravan and opened the door.

'I'll make you some tea,' she called—and then Jimmy heard her give a scream of fright. He saw his mother come tumbling down the caravan steps, almost falling to the ground in her hurry.

'Jimmy! Wally! There's a man in Jimmy's bed!' she cried. 'Come and turn him out!'

'Whatever next!' said Mr Wally, and he and Jimmy and Lotta raced to the caravan. Wally shot up the steps, and Jimmy followed.

Sure enough there was someone in Jimmy's bed! The bed-clothes were humped up in the middle, and there was a gentle sound of snoring.

Jimmy was angry. Who was this that dared to get into his own lovely bed and sleep there? He ripped off the clothes—and then he and Wally shouted with laughter!

It was Sammy the chimpanzee who was there! And he had undressed himself and put on Jimmy's own pyjamas, though they were very small for him! He had brushed his hair with a scrubbing brush, and then curled up in Jimmy's bunk. He loved Jimmy, and when the groom had frightened him, he had slipped out of the cage and gone to find the little boy.

The caravan door had been shut, but Sammy had hopped in through the open window. He was safe!

'Mother! It's only Sammy!' said Jimmy, roaring with laughter, whilst Lotta danced round on one leg, squealing and giggling.

But Mrs Brown was not pleased. 'I put clean sheets on that bed this morning!' she said indignantly. 'You bad chimpanzee, get up at once!'

So Sammy got up, took off Jimmy's pyjamas, and solemnly dressed himself again, keeping one eye on Mrs Brown, who was really quite annoyed.

'I like chimpanzees,' she said to Mr Wally, 'but *not* in my beds!'

'Very good, ma'am,' said Mr Wally meekly, and he went off with Sammy, whilst Jimmy and Lotta had fits of giggles all the time they were eating their tea!

'Really!' said Mrs Brown, 'you never know what's going to happen next in a circus!'

The Circus Does Well

The circus went very merrily at Westsea, and Mr Galliano took the big field for one more week. Everybody was pleased, for a great deal of money was taken at the gate.

'I shall be able to get my caravan painted again,' said Stanley the clown, 'and I'll get myself a new suit too. One with a tail sewn on.'

'A *tail*!' said Lotta. 'Whatever do you want a tail for? I've never heard of a clown with a tail before.'

"That's just why I thought I'd have one,' said Sticky Stanley, with a grin. 'Think what fun you'll all have in the ring, trying to pull my tail! I'll be Sticky Stanley, the only clown in the world with a tail!'

'He sticks to his work and his friends stick to him!' said Lotta, giving the smiling little man a hug, for she was very fond of him. 'You get your tail, Stanley, and we'll do plenty of pulling!'

So Stanley bought himself a marvellous new suit, and it had a long tail like a cow's that dragged along behind him, and was always tripping him up when he turned round to go another way. Lucky thought the tail was great fun, and one night in the ring she ran after Stanley and worried his tail as if it were a rat. Stanley slumped about, and yelled, and shouted, for he really was afraid that the dog would bite it off!

Of course all the watching people thought that it was part of the show, and they laughed till they cried. So the clown thought he had better let Lucky do it again each night.

'But mind you, Jimmy, you'll have to buy me a new tail if Lucky *does* happen to bite it off one night!' said the clown. 'Or else she'll have to give me her own. I wouldn't mind a tail like Lucky's, with a fine wag in it!'

Mr Galliano paid Jimmy quite a lot of money that week, and the little boy was overjoyed. It was wonderful to think that he and his clever little dog could earn so much. He saved half of it, and bought his mother a new dress, his father a new saw, and Lotta a fine pair of shoes, which she wore to please Jimmy, though she really preferred to run barefoot.

Mr Galliano began to think of engaging some new performers for the circus. Lotta's mother and father had taken their performing terriers with them, and they would not be back for some time. The circus was doing so well that it would be a good idea to make it even better.

'What shall we have next?' he asked his wife, kindly Mrs Galliano. 'We have monkeys, an elephant, a chimpanzee, Lucky the dog, and our dancing horses. We might get some performing seals, perhaps—yes?'

'Yes,' said Mrs Galliano. 'Write to Philippo and see if he will join our circus with his six performing seals. They are wonderful. They can balance long poles on their noses, they can play catch-ball, and they sit on stools and sway themselves in time to the music in a very marvellous way.'

When Jimmy and Lotta heard that perhaps the six performing seals might join the circus, they were most excited.

'I saw them once!' said Lotta. 'They are nice creatures, Jimmy, and they love doing tricks, just as the monkeys and Lucky do, and just as the horses love waltzing to the music!'

'I've never found out yet how those horses manage to dance round in time to the music,' said Jimmy seriously. 'Sometimes the music goes slow, and sometimes it goes fast—however do the horses follow it?'

'Jimmy!' cried Lotta, in surprise. 'Have you been with the circus all these months, and don't know that little trick yet?'

'What little trick?' asked Jimmy, astonished. 'Is there a trick?'

'Of course there is!' said Lotta, laughing. 'The horses don't dance in time to the music! The music keeps in time with *them*! That's why it sometimes goes slow and sometimes fast, silly! It keeps in time with the horses, the horses don't keep in time with the music!'

'Well, I never!' said Jimmy, amazed. 'I didn't know that before.'

'I do hope those seals come,' said Lotta, dancing about. 'We'll have fun with them, Jimmy.'

But it was most disappointing, they didn't come. Mr Philippo had joined another circus, and was not free to come to Mr Galliano. The children were sorry.

'I wonder what he *will* get,' said Lotta.

'Cats, perhaps,' said Jimmy.

'Pooh, cats!' said Lotta scornfully. 'Don't you know that cats can't perform? At least, they *won't* perform—not unless they're big cats, anyway.'

'Big cats?' said Jimmy. 'What sort of big cats? Fat ones, do you mean?'

Lotta went off into peals of laughter, and rolled on the grass. 'You *are* funny, Jimmy,' she said. 'Don't you know that big cats are tigers, or panthers, or some animal of that family? They are all cats. They purr like cats too. Haven't you heard them?'

'No,' said Jimmy. 'I've never even seen a real tiger or lion, except in pictures. But I'd like to. They look such great, magnificent creatures.'

Well, Jimmy was soon to see some real big cats, for Mr Galliano heard from two people called Roma and Fric, who owned six great tigers.

He showed the letter to Mrs Galliano, and he called Mr Tonks, Jumbo's keeper, into the caravan, and Lilliput, who owned the four monkeys, and Mr Wally, who owned Sammy the chimpanzee.

'I have a letter here, yes,' said Mr Galliano. 'It is from Roma and Fric, who have six tigers. They can sit on stools, jump through hoops, and play follow-my-leader. You have heard of them—yes?'

'I don't like trained cats, whether they are tigers, lions, leopards, or lynxes,' said Mr Wally. 'It isn't natural for cats to act.'

'They don't like it,' said Lilliput. 'They're not like monkeys, who act all the time, nor yet like Jumbo, who was bred and born in a circus.'

'It's a job to have travelling tigers,' said Mr Tonks, scratching his head. 'For one thing, we've got to have a mighty strong cage built each night in the ring before the tigers can do their turn, and that takes time.'

'Brownie can help with that—yes?' said Mr Galliano. 'We are going next to Liverpool, and Roma and Fric can join us there. Of course, people

'I don't like trained cats,' said Mr Wally.

like to see performing tigers—it looks dangerous, yes!'

'I don't like trained cats, big or little,' said Mr Wally again. 'But if people want to see them, I suppose circuses have got to have them. Give me animals that enjoy learning—tigers don't! It hurts their feelings.'

Very soon the news went round the camp. Performing tigers were to join the circus at Liverpool. Lotta and Jimmy were thrilled. 'Now I shall get to know tigers too,' said Jimmy happily, for he was a boy who loved and welcomed any animal, big or small. 'I wish I knew all the animals in the world!'

'You're a funny fellow, Jimmy,' said Mr Tonks, pulling the little boy's ear gently. 'I believe you would even love performing fleas! It's wonderful how all the animals take to you.'

Jimmy went red with pride. 'I shall make friends with the tigers too,' he said.

'Don't be too sure about that,' said Mr Tonks. 'Tigers are funny things, and not to be trusted. I reckon they ought never to be in a circus. They won't make friends with anyone—not real friends, like old Jumbo there, or Sammy the chimp.'

'Well, we'll see, Tonky,' said Jimmy, and he ran off to give Lucky a bath before her turn in the circus that night.

The show at Westsea finished that weekend, and soon the circus was on the move again, travelling towards Liverpool. It poured with rain as they went, and the children sat inside their caravan, and looked out on the dreary surroundings. They did not like the look of Liverpool very much, after the freedom and beauty of Westsea.

'But never mind, Lotta!' said Jimmy, jigging in joy. 'We shall meet the tigers at Liverpool! That will be a big treat, won't it!'

The Tigers Join the Circus

The circus camped before it got into Liverpool itself. The field was wet and muddy. It was hard work getting the tents up, and dragging the cages and caravans to their right place. Jumbo was very useful, but even his big feet slipped in the mud.

'The tigers aren't here yet,' said Jimmy to Lotta, in disappointment.

'No, they are coming tomorrow,' said Lotta. 'Mrs Galliano told me.'

The children were wet through when at last everything was in order that night. They went into their cosy caravan, and Mrs Brown made them take off their wet things and get into dry ones. Jimmy rubbed Lucky dry too, but Lulu the spaniel did not need to be dried, for she had kept in the caravan in her basket all the time. She loved Mrs Brown very much and liked to be near her.

Mrs Brown had a fine-smelling stew in a pan on the stove. The children sniffed hungrily. Mr Brown was pleased to smell it too when he came up the caravan steps to his supper. He took off his wet coat, washed his hands and face, and sat down at the little table. Soon everyone was enjoying the delicious stew, the chunks of pineapple that followed, and the hot cocoa.

'Ooh, isn't it cosy here,' said Jimmy. 'Who would live in a house when they could live in a caravan!'

'Well, I've never really got used to a caravan,' said Mrs Brown, pouring out the cocoa. 'It still seems funny to me not to have an upstairs and a downstairs. But I must say this is a very fine roomy caravan, Jimmy, almost as good as Mr Galliano's.'

'I love it,' said Lotta, sipping her cocoa. 'I miss my father and mother, Lal and Laddo, but I do love living with you and Brownie and Jimmy, Mrs Brown.'

'And we love having you, Lotta,' said Mrs Brown, smiling at the black-haired little girl. 'You are very useful to me in lots of ways—but you still haven't learnt that your hair looks nicer when it is properly brushed, and that toothbrushes are meant to be used!'

'Even Sammy the chimpanzee knows that,' said Jimmy, grinning. 'You'd better take a lesson from him, Lotta.'

Lotta made a dreadful face at Jimmy, and gave him such a pinch that the little boy yelled and dropped a piece of pineapple out of his open mouth.

'And *you'd* better go and learn manners from Sammy,' said Lotta rudely. 'Spitting out that nice pineapple!'

'I didn't!' cried Jimmy indignantly. You made me yell and it fell out of my mouth. I wonder where it went.'

'Lulu ate it,' said Mrs Brown. 'Now, no more faces and no more pinching, Lotta. You know I don't like it.'

'I've had to get in a lot of new bars and bolts,' said Mr Brown. 'Mr Galliano wants me to make the tigers' cage as strong as I can—the one they'll perform in, I mean.'

'Oooh, the tigers!' said Jimmy eagerly. 'I am longing to see them!'

The next day, as the children were practising in the ring with Lucky, ready for that night, they heard a strange new sound. Lucky pricked up her ears and listened, then put her tail down and crept between Jimmy's legs. Lulu ran out of the big tent and tore back to Mrs Brown for safety. Jumbo pricked his big ears at the bellowing noise, and the four monkeys and Sammy sat still and listened.

'The tigers!' yelled Jimmy in delight. 'I can hear them roaring! Come on, Lotta, let's go and meet them!'

The two children rushed into the wet field. At the gate was a great travelling-box, shut in on all sides, but with air-holes in the roof. It was a powerful motor-van, and its wheels churned up the mud of the field.

'It's stuck!' cried Jimmy. 'No wonder the tigers are bellowing! They can't understand what's happening! Let's go and tell Tonky, and perhaps old Jumbo will help to pull the van out of the mud. Hi, Mr Tonks! Mr Tonks!'

Mr Tonks was already undoing Jumbo's rope. Jumbo did not want to go near the van, for he disliked tigers, but he would do anything in the world for Mr Tonks. So he followed his keeper, and easily pulled the travelling cage from the deep mud.

The cage, full of roaring tigers, was hauled to its place in the field. Two people were with the cage, one a great powerful man with strange eyes, and the other a boy about Jimmy's age.

'Hallo,' said Jimmy. What's your name?'

'Fric,' said the boy, eyeing Jimmy carefully. 'And that's Roma over there, my uncle. I travel with him, and we manage the tigers together. What do you do?'

'I'm Jimmy, and I have a performing dog called Lucky,' said Jimmy proudly.

The boy looked interested. 'I've heard of her,' he said. 'She can walk the tight-rope and spell and count, can't she? All a trick, I suppose?'

'No, she's really very, *very* clever,' said Jimmy. 'What do your tigers do? Can I make friends with them, do you think?'

'Don't talk rubbish,' said the boy scornfully. 'Nobody makes friends with tigers. They won't let you. I advise you not to go near them. I'd like to see that dog of yours, though. I like dogs.'

Jimmy was pleased. It would be fun for him and Lotta to have another boy in the camp. They could do lots of things together. Lotta stood staring at the boy, but Eric took no notice of her.

'I've got to go and help feed the tigers now,' said Fric. 'See you later!'

He went off. Lotta made a face. 'I don't like him,' she said.

'Why, you don't even know him yet,' said Jimmy. 'He says he likes dogs. It will be fun to have someone else to play with.'

'*I* don't want anyone else,' said Lotta sulkily. 'I don't like Fric.' She went off by herself, but Jimmy waited about by the tigers' van, wondering if he might see inside.

Soon one side was opened, and Jimmy saw the tigers. They were magnificent creatures, like

30

Soon one side opened, and Jimmy saw the tigers.

enormous cats, with great white whiskers, beautiful gleaming eyes, and shining coats. They were well-fed now, and lay peacefully against one another, two in each partition of the big cage. They blinked at Jimmy in silence.

'You lovely things,' said Jimmy, looking at their great green eyes. 'I'd like to feel your furry coats!'

'Don't you have anything to do with tigers,' said a warning voice nearby. 'They are not to be trusted. A chimpanzee's all right, and so is an elephant, and even a bear knows its friends—but tigers hate this circus life and won't be friends.'

It was Mr Wally, who had come up to see the tigers too. The two gazed through the bars at the quiet creatures. One tiger got up and paced to and fro on big silent paws.

'Just like the cat we used to have at home,' said Jimmy. 'I'd like to go and pet it!'

'Aren't you afraid of those great creatures?' asked Mr Wally, in astonishment.

'No', said Jimmy. 'I'm not afraid of any animal, Mr Wally. It's not that I'm brave—it's just that I seem to understand them and their feelings, and I want them to be friends with me.'

'Well, don't try being friends with tigers, that's all!' said Wally, and he went off to his caravan, thinking that Jimmy was the strangest boy he had ever known. All the animals in the circus loved that boy—ah, he was lucky, for that was a great gift, to be friends with animals of all kinds, wild or tame! Mr Wally would like to have had Jimmy's gift of friendliness—he could manage chimpanzees, but dogs he didn't understand, and as for tigers, why, he didn't even like the feel of them in the circus!

Jimmy stayed looking at the tigers. They looked back at him. One of them began to purr gently, just like a great cat.

'You'll be friends of mine before long,' said the little boy in the low, gentle voice he kept for animals. 'You just see! I'll be feeding you soon— yes, and brushing those lovely coats of yours! You just see!'

Bad Tempers

The six new tigers soon settled down in Mr Galliano's circus. They roared when they were hungry, but not very often at other times.

'How do you manage to tame tigers, Fric?' asked Jimmy, as he saw the small boy going to feed his six great cats one morning.

'We had all these when they were cubs,' said Fric. 'They were just like playful kittens then. It is not very difficult to train them when they are young— and the tricks they learn then they always remember when they are grown tigers. And they are afraid of me and of Roma, just as they were afraid when they were cubs. If I shout at them they cower down.'

'Afraid of you!' cried Jimmy. 'I think that's wrong, Fric. I don't think we should ever make animals afraid of us when we take them to live with us. Mr Galliano says that the finest trainers work by kindness.'

'Pooh!' said Fric scornfully, 'he doesn't know anything about tigers then. No one could be kind to tigers for long!'

Bad Tempers

Jimmy said nothing. He felt sure that Fric was wrong. The little boy looked at the slanting green eyes of the six beautiful animals. One of them began to purr as she looked at Jimmy.

'Hear that!' said Fric, astonished. 'That's Queenie, purring. She hardly ever does. She must like you, Jimmy. It's a funny thing, too, but whenever you're near their cage, they always seem to lie peaceful and quiet.'

Fric went into the tigers' cage to feed them. There was a double gate, and one was always shut if the other was open, so that no tiger could ever get out. Fric was not afraid of the tigers. He had lived all his life with Roma, his uncle, and knew all about the great animals.

With loud roars the tigers fell upon their enormous hunks of meat. They took no notice of Fric.

'Watch what happens when I shout at Queenie, and thump my fist into my hand!' shouted Fric. And before Jimmy could stop him, Fric had yelled angrily at Queenie and banged his fist into the palm of his left hand.

Queenie crouched down, her ears drooping, and her tail swinging slowly. She looked scared.

'Don't do that, Fric,' said Jimmy. 'Why should you yell at Queenie like that when she's done nothing wrong at all? That's the wrong way to treat animals!'

Fric looked cross. He threw the last piece of meat to the tigers. 'You may know all about dogs and elephants and chimpanzees,' he said sulkily, 'but you don't know a thing about tigers!'

Jimmy did not want to quarrel with Fric, for he badly wanted something—he wanted to go into the tigers' cage with Fric! Jimmy was not afraid of any animal; no, not even of a fierce tiger. But Lucky was afraid. Little dog Lucky wouldn't go near the cage, and Jimmy was glad. He did not want Lucky to slip between the bars. She would make a nice little dinner for six hungry tigers!

Roma, Fric's uncle, cleaned out the tigers' cage each day. Fric fed them. At night the great cage was moved near to the big tent or 'top' as all the circus folk called it, and a passage-way was made from the travelling cage to a strong cage that Brownie, Jimmy's father, built with Roma in the ring each night, whilst Sticky Stanley the clown and Oona the acrobat were doing clever and funny tricks to amuse the watching people.

Then the tigers walked down the passage-way and entered the cage in the ring. In this cage were set six stools—two small, two tall, and two taller still. Each tiger knew his stool, and leapt nimbly on to it, so that they sat in a row, like steps going up and down.

Both Roma and Fric went into the cage with the tigers. They were dressed alike, in red velvet suits, very tight, with short, sparkling cloaks, and both carried a long whip that they could crack as loudly as Mr Galliano could crack his.

'Aren't Roma and Fric clever with those tigers?' whispered Lotta to Jimmy. 'I don't know how they make those great beasts obey them like that! Look at Queenie jumping gracefully through that paper hoop, and breaking the paper as she goes through it!'

'And look at Basuka, on one of the high stools!' said Jimmy. 'He's going to jump through *two* hoops!'

He did—and everyone clapped the graceful jump. Basuka did not go back to his stool. He stood and glared at the people. Roma cracked his whip.

'Up, Basuka, up!' he shouted. But still Basuka stood and stared. Roma picked up a sharp-pointed iron bar and pricked Basuka with it. The big tiger growled, but jumped up to his stool at once.

'I wish Roma wouldn't do that,' said Jimmy. 'I bet I could have made Basuka go back, without hurting him. It's not fair.'

Fric took up his own smaller whip then, and cracked it three times. At once one tiger after another jumped down from the stools, and arranged themselves in a circle about small Fric.

'Around you go!' shouted the boy, and cracked his whip again. At once the tigers began to pad round in a circle till the whip cracked again. Then they turned themselves the other way and went round in a ring in the opposite direction. Everyone clapped.

'Up!' roared Roma—and up went every tiger again on to the stools. The whip cracked once more. The two tigers in the middle, sitting on the tallest stools, at once stood up on their hind legs and put their front paws against each other's. Down jumped the other four tigers and went in and out of the archway made by the two middle tigers. It was extraordinary to watch.

'Fric's clever, you know, Lotta,' said Jimmy. 'And he's not a bit afraid.'

'I don't like Fric,' said Lotta obstinately. 'If he can be unkind to tigers, his own special animals, he can be unkind in other ways. I don't like him.'

'Oh, please, Lotta, don't be silly,' said Jimmy. 'We can all three have fun together. Come for a walk with us tomorrow morning, after we've done our jobs.'

'All right,' said Lotta. 'But I don't want to.'

So the next morning Jimmy called across to Fric. 'Hi, Fric! Come for a walk when you've finished this morning?'

'Right!' said Fric. So Jimmy and Lotta went to Fric's caravan when they were ready, and the boy jumped down the steps. But when he saw Lotta, he pulled a face.

'She's not going with us, is she?' he said.

'Of course,' said Jimmy, surprised. 'Why not?'

'Then I shan't come,' said Fric. 'Girls are silly. Always giggling and saying stupid things.'

'Lotta doesn't say stupid things!' cried Jimmy angrily. 'She's a fine girl. She can ride any horse you like, and she knows far more about dogs than you know about tigers!'

This was not a wise thing to say to Fric. He scowled angrily, pulled his cap over his forehead, and stalked off without a word. Jimmy called after him:

'Fric! Don't be a donkey! Come along with us. I've got some money to buy ice-creams.'

Fric stopped and turned round. He loved ice-creams but did he love them enough to put up with Lotta's company?

'Oh, come on, Fric,' said Jimmy impatiently. 'Come, Lotta, we'll go after him.'

But now Lotta turned sulky! She swung round and stood with her back to Jimmy, and she stamped her foot in a temper. 'I'm not coming!' she said. 'If you think I'm going anywhere with that horrid boy, you're wrong. I don't like him. I won't go with him.'

'But, Lotta!' said Jimmy, 'please, please don't be silly. You know that I want to make friends with Fric so that I can go into the tigers' cage and get to know the six tigers. He won't let me if I'm not friends with him.'

'You and your old tigers!' said Lotta, with tears of rage running down her cheeks. 'I hate you all!' And the cross little girl ran like the wind to Oona's caravan and sat watching the acrobat, who was practising steadily for that night's show.

Jimmy was upset. How silly of Lotta to behave like that! Never mind, perhaps she would forget it all by the time he came back from his walk. He would go with Fric and talk to him about tigers, and buy him ice-creams.

But Fric, too, had gone off in a temper! Poor Jimmy stood looking round dolefully, all alone.

'Hello, hello, hello!' said Sticky Stanley the clown, turning cart-wheels all around Jimmy on hands and feet. 'You look like a hen left out in the rain! Come and help old Tonky rub Jumbo down with oil. He's got some cracks in his hide, and it's a big job, I can tell you, to oil *him* all over!'

'All right,' said Jimmy, cheering up, for he loved doing anything with the big kindly elephant. 'I'll come.'

So off he went with Lucky at his heels, puzzled and not very happy.

Jimmy and the Tigers

Lotta sulked for a long time. She would not be friends with Fric, and Fric called rude things after her whenever he saw her. Jimmy was angry about it, but he could not make up his mind to quarrel with Fric, for he knew that if he did, there would be no chance of him going into the tigers' cage.

'Fric, please don't be unkind to Lotta,' he said. But Fric only laughed, and thought out another rude thing to say to Lotta when next he met her.

Jimmy bought Fric dozens of ices, scores of bars of chocolate, bags of sweets, and even a fine toy aeroplane that Fric wanted. Each time Fric promised to allow Jimmy to come with him into the big cage, but every time he broke his word.

'No,' he said. 'I'd better not today, Jimmy. If Roma got to hear of it, he'd scold me. Besides, I guess Mr Galliano would be angry if he knew.'

'Fric, I keep telling you I'll take the blame if anything happens, and Roma or Mr Galliano find out,' said Jimmy, in despair. 'Look here, you shan't have a single ice-cream or sweet till you've kept your word. I'm tired of trusting you.'

Fric was alarmed. He didn't want his supply of goodies to stop, and yet he really was scared of letting Jimmy into the cage. He knew quite well that it was not right to allow any stranger inside, for the tigers were fierce and powerful, and could certainly not be trusted with anyone they did not know. Also, he was scared of his uncle. What would Roma say if he found out?

'Wait till the tigers know you better,' he said.

'But you said that last week!' said Jimmy. 'And they know me now as well as they possibly can, seeing that they are inside the cage and I am outside. Do you know, Queenie came and rubbed her great head against my hand when I put it inside the cage-bars yesterday?'

'I don't believe that,' said Fric at once, for this was a thing that Queenie had certainly never done to Fric or to Roma either. She was the least good-tempered of the six tigers.

'All right. Come and see her do it again!' said Jimmy. So the two of them went along to the great travelling cage in which the tigers lived, two in each partition. They stared at the little boys with their green, glinting eyes. Queenie purred, got up slowly and gracefully, and came across to the bars. Jimmy

43

put his hand inside. The great tiger pressed her head against the small hand, and purred even more loudly. Jimmy scratched her where her whiskers grew.

Fric stared, his eyes as round as pennies. 'Goodness me!' he said. 'I've never seen such a thing! Fancy old Queenie doing that! She once nearly snapped a man's hand off when he put it too near.'

'Well, *now* will you let me go inside the cage?' asked Jimmy, delighted.

'Look here, Jimmy, I'll let you in tonight, when everyone's asleep in their caravans,' promised Fric. 'You can creep up to our caravan, and put your hand inside the window. I'll leave the keys of the cage just inside, and you can take them quietly.'

'But aren't you coming too?' asked Jimmy, in surprise.

'Indeed I'm not!' said Fric. 'You can do it on your own. *I'm* not going to get into any trouble about it!'

Jimmy ran off to his dinner, his eyes bright and his cheeks glowing. Tonight! And by himself too! Oh, what a glorious adventure! He could hardly eat his dinner, he was so excited.

'Jimmy, whatever's the matter with you?' asked his mother. 'You look as if somebody has left you a fortune! Look at him, Lotta.'

But Lotta wouldn't look. She hardly spoke to Jimmy these days, and she was so quiet that Mrs

Brown was quite worried about her. Poor Lotta! She thought that Jimmy wanted Fric for a friend instead of her, and she was worried too, because she did so want to go into the ring again and ride one of the horses, and Juanita, Pepita, and Lou would not say she could. She was not at all happy.

Jimmy did not notice Lotta's unhappy face. He was much too thrilled about what would happen that night. He wondered if he should tell Lotta. Yes, he would!

'Lotta, I've got a secret to tell you,' he said after dinner, when they were rubbing down the horses together, with Lou whistling not far off.

'Is it anything to do with Fric?' asked Lotta.

'Yes, it is, partly,' said Jimmy. 'Listen, Lotta, he is—'

'I don't want to know any secret if Fric's in it,' said Lotta, in a horrid, cold voice. 'I don't like Fric, and I'm beginning not to like you either, Jimmy.'

Jimmy was most astonished. Really, what was happening to Lotta? But he could not bother himself to think about that now, for his head was full of the tigers.

That night Jimmy crept out of his own caravan very quietly, without waking his mother, father, or Lotta. Only Lucky knew, and she was tied up and could not follow. Lulu opened one eye and then went to sleep again.

Jimmy stole towards Fric's caravan. The window was open. He could hear Fric's uncle snoring inside. He stood on a wheel and put his hand inside the window. He could feel three big keys there. So Fric had kept his word this time! The little boy's heart beat fast. He carefully picked up the keys so that they did not make a single clink, and slipped down from the wheel.

He ran like a shadow to the tigers' great travelling-box. It was completely shut up. Air came in through the ventilating holes in the roof. There was not a sound from the cages inside.

Sammy the chimpanzee heard Jimmy's soft footsteps and made a little noise. But for once Jimmy paid no attention to Sammy. He came to the tigers' cages, and slipped a key into the lock. He turned the lock, opened the door, and slipped inside. There was another door to unlock inside, and then a gate of iron bars. Jimmy unlocked them all.

The tigers stirred and awoke. Jimmy could see two pairs of green eyes glinting in the dark. Moonlight came filtering in through the air-holes in the roof.

The two tigers in the first cage sniffed and growled a little. Then Queenie, one of the two tigers,

Jimmy spoke to the tigers in his special animal-voice.

lifted her head high and sniffed harder. Yes, this was the boy who so often came outside the cage and talked to her in that lovely, gentle voice. This boy had no whip, no iron bar. This boy had a voice that was gentle like the leaves, not fierce and harsh and frightening.

Jimmy stood inside the tigers' cage, his heart thumping against his side. He was not afraid. Jimmy had never in his life been afraid of any animal, and he never would be. But he was excited, and he felt sure that the tigers would hear his heart thumping and wonder what it was. He put his hand over his heart to hide the thumping.

Queenie began to purr. She left her corner and silently slunk over to Jimmy. She put her great head down beside his right arm. Jimmy spoke to her in his special animal-voice, strong, and low, and gentle.

'Old Queenie,' he said. 'Old Queenie, you beauty. You great, green-eyed, graceful tiger. You love me, don't you? And I love you. I love your grand head and your slanting eyes, your fine whiskers and your slinky body.'

Queenie purred more loudly. The other tiger looked on watchfully. She knew Jimmy, but she wanted Queenie to make sure he was friendly first.

'Ruby!' said Jimmy, calling the other tiger by her name. 'Ruby! Do you want your head rubbed, Ruby?'

But Ruby would not come near that first night. She lay peacefully, watching with her green eyes, whilst Queenie fussed round the little boy, nearly bowling him over when she pushed him playfully with her great head.

Jimmy did not go to the other tigers that night. He slipped out of Queenie's cage after about half an hour, very pleased with his first visit. The other tigers had been restless, smelling the scent of a strange visitor, but they had soon settled down when they heard Queenie purring.

'Tomorrow!' said Jimmy excitedly to himself, 'tomorrow night I shall go again, and I will go to *all* the tigers. The big beautiful things! They will soon be my friends. How *can* Fric be unkind to them? Why, Queenie was as loving as an old fireside tabbycat tonight!'

He slid into his caravan, and didn't know that Lotta was awake, wondering where he had been! He put his head down on the pillow, and was soon fast asleep.

Lotta Discovers Jimmy's Secret

Jimmy dreamt about tigers all that night! When he awoke in the morning he remembered how Queenie had made friends with him and rubbed her great head against him, purring all the time. Jimmy looked at Lotta, and wished he could tell her, but Lotta was very sulky and quiet these days.

Lotta was wondering where Jimmy had been the night before. What had made him slip out of bed all alone? She made up her mind to watch that night and follow Jimmy.

Fric ran across to Jimmy as the little boy was practising with Lucky for the night's show. Lucky was spelling out the word 'Galliano,' fetching each letter in turn in her mouth, and putting them down in a row.

'My word!' said Fric, stopping in amazement. 'That dog is a wonder, Jimmy! How did you teach her to spell and count? Did you have her as a puppy?'

'She's not much more than a puppy now!' said Jimmy proudly. 'Yes, I taught her every trick she knows, Fric. She's a naturally clever dog, and she loves learning. I'd never teach any animal that didn't want to learn, you know. That's why I'd never teach tigers. They don't want to learn.'

'I say, Jimmy, did you go into their cage last night?' asked Fric eagerly. 'Or were you afraid?'

'Afraid!' said Jimmy scornfully. 'Of course I wasn't! Yes, I went in, but only into the first partition. Ruby didn't come to me, but Queenie did. She purred all over me and rubbed herself against me like a cat!'

Fric stared. 'It's funny,' he said at last. 'I just don't understand it. I and Roma have had those tigers from cubs, and they know us and fear us. But you are a stranger. Why should they be friends with you?'

Jimmy laughed, and took up a brush to brush Lucky, though her coat already shone like satin. The little dog stood up on her hind legs when Jimmy wanted to brush her underneath.

'I'm going into *all* the cages tonight,' said Jimmy. 'Leave the keys near the caravan window again, Fric.'

'Well, you'll have to buy me an ice-cream today then,' said Fric greedily. So Jimmy promised, and Fric went off to give the tigers fresh water. Roma was already cleaning the cages out, whilst the tigers lay and watched the big broom sweeping.

That night Jimmy once more slipped out of his caravan at midnight, and, in the pale light of the moon, took the keys from the window of Fric's caravan, and ran across to the tigers' big travelling cage.

Someone saw him go. Someone followed him. Lotta slid like a shadow after Jimmy, wondering where he was going. How she hoped he was not going off with Fric somewhere, for the little girl hated Fric.

She was very frightened when she saw Jimmy going to the tigers' cage, and more frightened still when she saw him unlock the door and go inside,

'He'll be killed!' said the little girl to herself. 'I know he's clever with animals, but tigers are different. They're fierce and wild. He'll be killed!'

She did not dare to call out, for she was afraid of upsetting the tigers. But she slipped in at the first door and stood outside the inner gate of the cage, trying to see what Jimmy was doing.

By the faint light of the moon filtering in through the air-holes, Lotta could see Jimmy and Queenie and Ruby. And what she saw made her eyes open in astonishment!

Jimmy was tickling Queenie, the enormous tiger, who was lying on her back like a kitten, all four paws in the air. Ruby was pawing at Jimmy gently, asking for her turn. The little girl had never seen tigers behaving like that before. Usually they were sullen and fierce with human beings, but here were Queenie and Ruby playing like tame cats!

The tigers smelt her as she stood there, and turned their heads. But they knew her smell, and turned back to play with their friend Jimmy. Soon the little boy slipped into the next partition, and Lotta could no longer see him.

'He shouldn't do this, he shouldn't, he shouldn't,' said the little girl to herself. 'It's too dangerous. Suppose Jimmy stumbled over one of their paws or trod on a tail by mistake? They would turn on him, and he wouldn't have a chance of escape! Oh, what shall I do to stop him?'

She stood and waited, hoping that nothing would happen to Jimmy. 'If I tell Mrs Brown, Jimmy would never forgive me,' thought Lotta. 'And it's no use asking him not to go in, for he'd laugh at me. I know what I'll do! I'll go to Fric, and tell him I know all about this, and I'll say that if he lets Jimmy have the keys of the tigers' cage again, I'll tell Mr Galliano! He won't dare to after that! And I'll say that if he dares to tell Jimmy that I know, I'll tell his uncle.'

Jimmy was making friends with the other tigers. The big travelling-box echoed with the sound of happy purring, as all the tigers pawed at Jimmy to make him play with them, or came to him with heads down, rubbing against his side and legs. Jimmy put his arms round Basuka, the biggest tiger of all.

'You are a magnificent fellow, Basuka!' he said, in his low voice. 'I could make you do anything! But I never would, for you are too grand to do silly little tricks.'

Jimmy spent an hour in the tigers' cages, and then slipped out, happy and excited. The tigers were far more his friends than they were either Roma's or Fric's! He loved them and they loved him. Jimmy felt Queenie's warm breath on his face as he locked the inner gate. The big tiger did not want him to go. She wanted this understanding boy to stay with her.

Lotta slipped like a shadow back to her caravan and was in her bunk, pretending to be asleep, when Jimmy came back. She lay awake a long time, afraid that if she did not stop Jimmy going into the tigers' cages he would one night be badly hurt.

So the next day, when Jimmy was helping Tonks to water Jumbo the elephant, Lotta hunted out Fric. The boy scowled at her, for he did not like girls.

'I want to speak to you, Fric,' said Lotta.

'Well, I don't want to speak to *you*,' said Fric rudely, and he turned his back.

'Look here, Fric,' said Lotta desperately. 'If you let Jimmy go into the tigers' cages again, I'll tell Mr Galliano, so there!'

Fric spun round in a trice and glared at the little girl. 'What do you know about it?' he demanded.

'Never mind,' said Lotta. 'But I'm not going to have Jimmy hurt by those tigers of yours, just because you're greedy for ice-creams and give him the keys each night in return for things like that! So just you look out, you horrid little boy!'

Fric rushed at Lotta and scared her so much that she cried out. Stanley the clown saw them and he came up.

'Stop it, Fric,' he said sternly. 'Lotta, go back to your caravan.' So, before anything else could be said, the two were separated, and Lotta went sobbing back to her caravan, glad that nobody was there to see her.

But she was not there long before Jimmy came rushing up with news.

'Lotta! Lilliput is ill! He's eaten something bad, and he's got a dreadful pain. I'm going for the doctor. Look after Jemima for him, will you?'

Jimmy rushed off, and Lotta ran to Lilliput's caravan. She was very fond of the little man and his four monkeys. Jemima was his pet, and was like a mischievous child.

Lilliput was lying on his bunk inside his caravan, very white indeed. Jemima was sitting at the head of the bed, looking doleful, for she could not understand what was wrong with her master.

'Are you ill, Lilliput?' said Lotta kindly. 'Jimmy's gone for the doctor. Does Mr Galliano know?'

Lilliput nodded feebly. At that moment heavy feet came up the steps at the back of the caravan, and Mr Galliano put his head in.

'You cannot go in the ring tonight, Lilliput—no?' he said kindly. 'You will be better soon—yes?'

Lilliput nodded. 'I'd like Lotta to take care of Jemima for a day or two,' he said. 'It's not good for her to be in here with me when I'm ill.'

'You will do so, Lotta—yes?' said Mr Galliano. The little girl picked up the small monkey and cuddled her. 'Yes,' she said. 'I'd love to look after her. She is fond of me and will be quite happy. I'll send Mrs Brown to see to you, Lilliput.'

'Well I don't want to speak to you,' said Fric rudely.

She slipped down the steps with Jemima curled round her neck like a fur, the monkey's tiny fingers holding on to her black curls. She ran to tell Mrs Brown, who had just come back from shopping, and Mrs Brown at once hurried to Lilliput's caravan to see what she could do.

Mr Galliano arranged for Mr Wally to take Lilliput's monkeys into the ring that night, for he was just as good with monkeys as with chimpanzees, and he knew exactly what to do with them. Lotta was to care for Jemima till Lilliput was better, and only when the circus was on each night was Jemima to leave the little girl, and go into the ring with the other three monkeys to do her funny tricks.

Fric saw Lotta in the distance with something round her neck, and he wondered what it was. He went nearer to see. 'Why, she's got Lilliput's Jemima!' he said, and he wondered why. He soon found out, and then the unkind boy made up his mind to punish Lotta for what she had said to him earlier that day!

'I'll get Jemima from her!' he thought. 'And I'll hide the monkey somewhere where she can't find it. That will give her a shock! That will teach her to come and say she'll tell Mr Galliano about me!'

He could not get Jemima that day, for Lotta was near her own caravan. Nor could he tell Jimmy what Lotta had said, for the little boy was busy the whole day long. He passed Fric once, and whispered to him:

'Shan't want the keys tonight, Fric. I'll have them again tomorrow. I'm tired today, with two late nights.'

Fric nodded, and had no time to say anything more. 'Wish I could get my chance to get Jemima away from Lotta!' he thought.

His chance came the next day. And Fric took it, though afterwards he very much wished that he hadn't.

Oh, Poor Little Jemima

Lilliput was a little better the next day, but he would not be able to go into the ring for four days, the doctor said. So Lotta was to have Jemima, his best-loved monkey, till he was well. The little girl was delighted, for Jemima was very sweet and loving.

Mrs Brown was not quite so delighted, for Jemima was the most mischievous monkey in the world! When Mrs Brown scolded her for taking down all the cups from the shelf and hiding them under the pillows, Jemima picked up some potatoes and threw them very quickly at the astonished Mrs Brown.

Lotta stopped her at once, and laughed till the tears came into her eyes. Jemima jumped on to the little girl's shoulder and nibbled her ear gently. That was one of her ways of loving anyone.

'Where's Jimmy?' asked Lotta. But Mrs Brown didn't know. Lotta wondered whether he was near the tigers' cage, so off she went, with Jemima curled round her neck, chattering nonsense into her ear.

Jimmy was not there. Lotta stood watching the great tigers, the side of whose cage was open, so that they could get the warm spring sun. And it was just then that Fric saw Lotta and Jemima, and made up his mind to take the monkey from Lotta and hide her somewhere so that the little girl would not know where to find her!

The boy crept quietly up behind Lotta. Jemima heard him and turned her head, chattering angrily, for she did not like Fric. Fric caught hold of her and dragged the monkey off Lotta's shoulder. The little girl screamed and turned round.

She saw Fric running away, holding the screaming monkey. 'Fric! Fric! Give me back Jemima!' cried the little girl. 'You wicked boy!'

But Fric only laughed. 'I'll teach you to order me about!' he yelled. But just then Jemima bit his hand as hard as she could with her sharp monkey-teeth and the boy shouted in pain. The monkey took her chance and struggled free. Frightened out of her life, she scampered round the tigers' cage, followed by Fric, who was roaring angrily.

The tigers pricked up their ears, and Queenie growled. No tiger likes disturbance and noise.

Jemima scampered round again, with Fric after her. 'Come to me, Jemima, come to me!' called Lotta. But the monkey was too afraid to pay any attention to Lotta.

And then a dreadful thing happened! Fric almost caught the monkey, and in fright the little thing ran up the bars of the tigers' cage and dropped inside

'Oh! Oh!' wailed Lotta 'They'll kill Jemima! They'll kill her!'

Fric stopped, frightened. Jemima ran to the back of Queenie's cage. Queenie growled. Scared, Jemima ran up the dividing bars between Queenie's cage and the next. The big tigers watched her. All of them were upset now, for the shouting and running and squealing had made them restless and angry.

'Jemima, oh, Jemima, do come here to me,' sobbed poor Lotta. 'Fric, make your tigers lie down.'

But Fric could not do anything with the tigers when they were angry. He just stood and stared, with his face suddenly rather pale. He knew that Jemima was a valuable monkey and that Lilliput loved her as if she were a child.

Jemima ran about Queenie's cage, scared. She did not dare to come out whilst Fric stood outside. All the tigers were up now, and were pacing their cages, their tails swinging and their big heads down.

Queenie put out a great paw and struck at the monkey as she fell.

Round and round they went, round and round, sniffing the strange monkey-smell of Jemima, disturbed and angry.

Then Queenie roared, and poor Jemima fell in fright from her place half-way up the cage-bars. In a trice Queenie put out a great paw and struck at the little monkey as she fell. Jemima tumbled with a little thud to the floor of the cage, and lay there, her brown monkey-eyes closed. She did not move.

Poor Lotta was almost mad with despair. She rubbed the tears from her cheeks, and looked round for help. 'Jemima will be eaten!' she wailed. 'Oh, where's Roma? He must go into Queenie's cage and save Jemima before the tigers do anything else to her.'

Mr Galliano came up, frowning, wondering what all the fuss was about. 'Mr Galliano, look, look, poor little Jemima is in Queenie's cage, and Ruby is there too, and they've hurt her and will eat her if we don't save her!' cried the little girl. 'Get Roma, oh, please, get Roma quickly, Mr Galliano!'

Mr Galliano saw what was happening at once. He cracked his big whip like a pistol-shot, three times. This was the signal for everyone to come to him at once. From every caravan and cage, from the stables and from all corners of the field, men and women came running.

'Roma!' shouted Galliano. 'Where's Roma?'

'Here!' shouted the big, powerful tiger-tamer, and he rushed up. 'What's wrong?'

'Lilliput's monkey is in your cage,' said Mr Galliano. 'Go in and get her out before the tigers eat her.'

Roma looked at the angry tigers, pacing their cages, snarling and growling. He looked at Queenie, who was standing over the still monkey, sniffing at her.

'Go on in,' commanded Mr Galliano. 'You aren't afraid, surely!'

'Don't you go in, Uncle!' shouted Fric suddenly. 'You know what Queenie is when she's in a temper! She'll spring at you!'

'I can't go in, Mr Galliano,' said Roma. 'If it was any other tiger but Queenie, I would, but Queenie's not to be trusted.'

Just then someone staggered up—it was Lilliput, who, hearing the three cracks of Galliano's whip, had hurriedly dragged on a dressing-gown and somehow got down his caravan steps, and come to see what was the matter. When he saw his beloved monkey, Jemima, lying quite still inside the tigers' cage, he gave a loud yell.

'Jemima! My little Jemima!' he cried. 'Get her out! Roma, Fric, go and get her out! What are you waiting for? Do you want to see her eaten?'

'No one can go in whilst Queenie is like that,' said Roma sullenly.

Lilliput gazed at his much-loved monkey, and the tears ran down his white cheeks. He tied his dressing-gown girdle firmly round him and turned to Roma.

'Give me the keys,' he commanded. '*I'll* go in! I'll get Jemima. I don't care twopence for your tigers!' Roma shook his head, but Lilliput made a dart at him and snatched the keys from Roma's belt. He ran like lightning to the door of the cage. But Galliano was there like lightning too! He pulled the little man back firmly.

'No,' he said, 'no, Lilliput. Your monkey may be dear to you, yes, but you also are dear to us! We cannot have you giving yourself to the tigers, no. Go back to your caravan, yes, and we will do what we can.'

Lilliput fought against Galliano, but he was small and the ring-master was big. Whilst this was going on there came the sound of pattering footsteps and panting breath, and up ran Jimmy. He had been taking Lucky for a walk and had only just come back. When he saw the crowd around the tigers' cage he knew something was wrong, and he had run to find out.

'What's up?' he cried, and then he saw Jemima, lying quite still, with Queenie standing over her, growling and snarling.

'Oh, Jimmy, Roma won't go in; he's afraid,' cried Lotta. 'What can we do?'

'Do!' cried Jimmy at once. 'Why, *I'll* go in of course! Roma, where are the keys?'

Everyone fell silent when they heard Jimmy's clear voice shouting that he would go into the cage. Galliano turned and smiled.

'No, Jimmy,' he said. 'You may be good with dogs and chimps and elephants, but with tigers, no! You will not go in!'

'Mr Galliano, sir,' cried Jimmy, 'didn't I go and rescue Jumbo when he got lost in the storm? Didn't I find Sammy the chimpanzee when he ran away, and bring him back? Well, let me save Jemima! I'm not afraid of the tigers. They are all friends of mine.'

Then Lotta spoke. 'Jimmy has already been in the tigers' cage,' she said. 'They love him.'

Roma stared in amazement and anger. Galliano pursed up his thick lips and looked at Jimmy. 'You are a strange boy, yes!' he said. 'I do not know whether to let you or not.'

'Queenie! Queenie!' Jimmy said suddenly, turning to the big tiger. 'What a noise to make! I don't
like it! Come now, come!'

When the big tiger heard the clear, low voice she
loved, she raised her head and sniffed. She pressed
her head against the strong bars and Jimmy pulled
her whiskers gently. The great tiger purred.

'It is enough,' said Galliano. 'You may go in,
Jimmy—but get the hoses out first, Oona and
Stanley, and be ready to turn on the water at the first
sign of danger!'

Oona and Stanley hurried to get the hose-pipes.
Hosing tigers and lions with water when they
became fierce was often a harmless way of making
them docile and tame once more. Mr Galliano
arranged for the water to be turned on should the
tigers growl at Jimmy when he was in the cage.
Then the boy could slip out in safety whilst the
tigers were scared of the water.

'Lotta, get a net on a long handle,' ordered Jimmy,
taking the keys from Lilliput, who was still sobbing.
'I'll get Queenie and Ruby to the back of the cage,
and you must gently put the net over Jemima and
pull her quietly out between the bars.'

'Good idea, yes!' said Mr Galliano, watching the
tigers closely. The hoses were brought up and
pointed at the cage in case they should be needed.

68

Jimmy unlocked the first cage-door, shut it, and unlocked the second. He walked into the tigers' cage and looked at the two green-eyed, angry animals, whose tails were swinging slowly to and fro like a restless cat's.

'Queenie!' said Jimmy softly, standing where he was, and not making any more movement. 'Queenie! Ruby! Lovely things, aren't you! Do you want to be rubbed? Do you want to be tickled?'

Queenie looked at the boy and purred. Ruby growled softly. Jimmy went on talking. 'Come, Queenie! You must come to me. Come here. Come close. Ruby, come here. Come and smell me. I am your friend, Jimmy.'

Jimmy spoke to the tigers without stopping, always in that low, gentle voice of his that all animals seemed to love. Queenie sniffed at Jemima, and then looked at Jimmy.

'Come, Queenie, come, come,' said Jimmy, and still he made no movement. Everyone stood watching in silence. Would Jimmy really be able to save poor little Jemima?

Mr Galliano is Angry

Jimmy still stood at the back of the tigers' cage. He did not even stretch out his hand, but his gentle voice went on and on, talking to the two tigers whilst they watched him.

'Don't you want your head to be rubbed, Queenie? Don't you want your ears stroked, Ruby? Then come to me.'

All the other tigers in the farther cages had stopped pacing round and round as soon as they heard Queenie purring. Basuka, hearing Jimmy's voice, began to purr too. All the tigers gradually became quieter. And still Jimmy's low voice went on and on and on. It seemed to Lotta that it had some sort of magic in it. Everyone had to listen. Everyone seemed to feel that they too wanted to go to Jimmy, and be stroked! It was very strange.

Queenie suddenly went over to Jimmy and pressed her great head lovingly against the little boy, almost knocking him over. She purred so loudly that even Basuka's purr could not be heard! Jimmy put out his hand and rubbed Queenie's great head. Ruby turned her back on the watching people and stared unwinkingly at the small boy.

This was Lotta's chance. Cautiously the little girl lifted the long-handled net that Oona had found and pushed into her hand. Slowly, without a sound, the net was held closer and closer to the cage. It was pushed through the bars—it was placed gently over the still monkey!

Then gently the little girl pulled the net back, and Jemima came with it! Ruby turned just as the monkey was drawn out of the cage. Lotta twisted the net round quickly so that Jemima did not fall out, and in a trice Jemima was in Lilliput's arms and he was rocking her like a baby.

Ruby was startled. She roared, and Galliano called to Jimmy, 'Out, boy! Out, quickly!'

But Jimmy laughed. He went up to the roaring tiger and looked her in the eyes. He put his arm round her neck and pressed his face against her furry cheek. The great tiger purred happily, and suddenly rolled over on to her back to be tickled like a cat!

'He could do anything with those tigers of mine!' muttered Roma to himself. 'I would like that boy. He is far, far better than Fric! Those tigers would clean his boots for him if he told them to. What a boy that is!'

Mr Galliano spoke again. 'I said, come out, Jimmy, yes!' he said. And there was something in his voice that made the little boy obey at once. He gave a parting rub to Ruby and a pat to Queenie, and then slipped out of the little cage-gate. He locked it, and unlocked the outer door. He slipped out of that, and locked it.

And then how everyone came round him and patted him and praised him. But somebody was crying! And that was Mrs Brown, Jimmy's mother, who had not dared to say a word whilst Jimmy was rescuing Jemima, but was now so glad to see Jimmy safe that she could not help crying.

'Now, now, Mrs Brown,' said Oona the acrobat, patting her shoulder. 'You should be proud of Jimmy, not cry tears all down his neck.'

'If this sort of thing is going to happen often, I declare I won't stay in the circus!' wept Mrs Brown, really upset, 'I'm not used to a circus life. I'm not used to all these scares!'

'Mother, I was quite safe!' said Jimmy. 'I could do anything with those tigers. What about Jemima? How is she?'

Lilliput had taken the little monkey back to his caravan. He had given her half a teaspoonful of brandy, and the little monkey had opened her eyes. She clutched Lilliput with her tiny hands, and trembled, for she had been very frightened. Lilliput

72

Mr Galliano is Angry

'You will tell me your tale—yes?' said Mr Galliano.

talked to her and soothed her, stroking her soft little brown head. He had forgotten he was ill. He thought only of his beloved little monkey.

'She is not hurt—no?' said Mr Galliano, looking into the caravan. 'Just her fright and the tumble, poor beast. Give her some hot milk, Lilliput. She will soon forget. How did she come to get into the tigers' cage? You can tell me—yes?'

'Ask Lotta,' said Lilliput, not looking up. 'She said something about that boy Fric.'

Galliano sent Sticky Stanley to fetch Lotta, Fric, and Jimmy. All three came to his caravan, looking rather scared, for Mr Galliano did not usually send for anyone unless he had a scolding for them.

Mrs Galliano sat in the caravan, mending Galliano's enormous socks. Galliano sat at the table, drumming on it with his hand. The three children came up the steps and stood in front of him.

'You will each tell me your tale—yes?' said Mr Galliano. 'You first, Fric. And the truth, please.'

Fric did not want to tell Mr Galliano anything, but as he felt sure that the ring-master already knew the truth, he thought it was better to tell it.

'I saw Lotta carrying Jemima on her shoulder,' he said sulkily. 'I don't like Lotta, so I thought I would give her a fright. I snatched Jemima away—and the monkey bit me, so I had to let her go. She ran into the tigers' cage, and when I saw that the tigers were angry I didn't dare to go in and get her.'

'So!' said Mr Galliano, his face one big frown. 'You do not like someone, no, so you get a little monkey into trouble, one who had done you no harm! You are a bad boy, yes. Now you, Lotta, speak. How is it that Fric does not like you?'

'He doesn't like me because I knew that he let Jimmy have the keys of the tigers' cage at night,' said Lotta, in a low voice. 'And I said I would tell you, Mr Galliano, if he did not stop giving Jimmy the keys, because I was so afraid the tigers might hurt Jimmy. He isn't a real circus boy, and he wouldn't know that tigers are not to be trusted.'

'So!' said Mr Galliano again, his eyebrows lifted so high that they nearly disappeared into his thick black hair. 'And now you, Jimmy? What have you to say?'

Jimmy was very red. He began to feel that it was partly his fault that Jemima had been so nearly killed. If he hadn't made Fric give him the keys, then Lotta wouldn't have been frightened about him, and wouldn't have spoken to Fric like that—and Fric wouldn't have tried to upset Lotta by snatching poor Jemima away.

'Mr Galliano, sir,' he said, 'it's quite true. I did get Fric to give me the keys. I knew Roma would never let me into the cage if I asked him. And I went in at night and made friends with all the tigers.'

'Such a thing is not allowed in any circus, no,' said Mr Galliano sternly. 'A careless boy might let all the tigers out, or, if he were not so clever as you with animals, he might be badly hurt, yes! You have saved Jemima, through your friendship with the tigers, so I will say no more but this. You will promise me, Jimmy, in the future never to enter any animal's cage unless you have my permission. That is understood—yes?'

'Yes, Mr Galliano,' said Jimmy meekly. 'May I go on making friends with the tigers, please, sir?'

'You must ask Roma,' said Mr Galliano. Then he turned to sulky Fric. 'As for you,' he said, 'you need a punishment, yes! I shall tell Roma to scold you well. Then perhaps you will think twice before you put an animal into danger—yes?'

'Yes, Mr Galliano,' said Fric, upset, because he knew that his uncle had a bad temper.

'Now go,' said Galliano, waving them out. 'You are more trouble than all the grown-ups put together, that is certain, yes!'

The three children went out silently. Fric ran off by himself. Jimmy took Lotta's hand. 'Don't worry, Lotta,' he said. 'I did try to tell you my secret about going into the tigers' cage, but you wouldn't listen. Cheer up! It's all right now.'

Lotta made one of her dreadful faces, and squeezed Jimmy's arm. 'Well, you won't want to be friends with that horrid boy any more,' she said happily. 'That's one good thing! Let's go and see how Lilliput and Jemima are.'

They were quite all right. Lilliput seemed better, except that his legs felt a bit weak. Jemima was sitting on his bed, drinking milk out of her little tin mug, chattering away to Lilliput in monkey-language. She had a bruise on her back where Queenie had struck her, but it was not very bad. She was wearing a blue ribbon round her neck and was very proud of it.

'She's fine,' said Lilliput to Jimmy. 'Jimmy, I'll never be able to thank you properly for saving Jemima. You're the finest boy I know! You come to me whenever you need any help, and you'll always get it.'

'Thank you, Lilliput,' said Jimmy, petting Jemima, whilst Lotta peeled a grape for the tiny monkey. 'I don't expect I'll need any help, though!'

But that's just where Jimmy was wrong, as you will see!

Goodbye to the Tigers

The show at Liverpool came to an end, and once again the tents were taken down, the caravans had their horses put between the shafts, and there was a great deal of noise and shouting. The tigers roared, for they hated any disturbance, and once Jimmy went into their cages with Roma to quiet them.

Roma looked at the quiet little boy, and spoke to him. 'Would you like to join me?' he asked. 'You are wonderful with the tigers, Jimmy. If anything should ever happen to your dog, Lucky, you come to me, and I will find a place for you with the tigers.'

'No, thank you, Roma,' said Jimmy at once. 'For one thing, nothing will happen to Lucky, for I am very careful of her—and for another, I shouldn't care to train tigers. They are not the right kind of animals for tricks. They don't enjoy them. I only like teaching animals that love to learn.'

'You speak stupidly,' said Roma, offended. 'It is a grand thing to be a tiger or lion tamer.'

'Well,' said Jimmy, 'it's not the sort of grand thing I like to do. I love going into the ring with Lucky! I'd much rather go with her than with tigers.'

'It is true she is a marvellous dog,' said Roma. 'You should sell her for a lot of money, Jimmy, and buy more dogs. Then you would have a whole troupe!'

'Sell her!' said Jimmy, amazed. 'I wouldn't sell Lucky for anything. Why, I love her!'

Fric was nearby, listening. He would not speak to Jimmy nowadays, for he blamed Jimmy and Lotta for the scolding Roma had given him. He was a spiteful little boy and would dearly have loved to pay Jimmy back. But he did not see how to.

The circus moved off to its next showplace in Greenville. This was a much more countrified place than outside Liverpool, and Jimmy and Lotta were pleased. It was early summer now, and camping out was very pleasant. It was grand to wake up in the morning and hear the birds singing, the cocks at the nearby farm crowing, and the murmur of the bees in the hawthorn hedges.

'The may is like snow, all over the hedge,' said Lotta, smelling it. 'Let's bathe in the stream when we go to get the water.'

Lotta ran barefoot again, and, Jimmy would have liked to, but his mother wouldn't let him. 'No,' she said firmly. 'You're not going to get into that kind of circus way, Jimmy. As for you, Lotta, run barefoot if you must, but don't forget to clean your teeth and brush your hair.'

Lotta was still not very good at keeping herself tidy enough for Mrs Brown, for she was a proper little circus girl, thinking that tidiness and prettiness were only to be kept for the ring at night. All the other circus folk thought so too, and they went about in the oddest clothes all day, except for Mr Galliano, who was always smart, and who, as his habit was, wore his top hat right on one side when the show went well!

Once he wore it so much to one side after a very good show that it fell off, and Jemima had sprung down to get it. She dashed off with it, and took it to Sammy the chimpanzee, who, very pleased indeed with such a fine hat, put it on, and walked all round the field with it! Everyone roared with laughter except Galliano himself, who was quite annoyed to see his fine top hat worn by a cheeky chimpanzee!

Once more the show opened, and the people of Greenville and all round flocked to see it. How they laughed at the funny antics of Sticky Stanley, how they clapped at the beautiful dancing horses, and stared at Sammy the chimpanzee and marvelled at the little dog Lucky!

They thought that the six tigers were marvellous too, and it made them shiver and shake when they saw Roma and Fric walk boldly into the cage in the ring. Jimmy had never been allowed to go into the ring with the tigers, though he often helped Roma.

'Soon I shall have your tigers curling round my feet like tame cats!' he said with a laugh. But Roma shook his head.

'We leave Mr Galliano's circus when this show is over,' he said. 'We are joining another circus, Jimmy. You will have to say goodbye to Queenie and Ruby and Basuka and the rest.'

Jimmy was sad. He had grown to love the green-eyed, graceful tigers. He wondered what other animals Mr Galliano would have next. He ran to ask Lotta if she knew.

'Yes,' said Lotta. 'Oona the acrobat has just told me. It's bears!'

'Bears!' said Jimmy. 'Ooooh! That will be fun!'

'Remember your promise to Mr Galliano, Jimmy,' said Oona the acrobat warningly, as he stood on his head outside his caravan, practising for that night's show.

'Yes,' said Jimmy, 'I won't forget. When will the bears come, Oona?'

'Not till we get to our next show-place,' said Oona, still balancing on his head, and working his legs above him as if he were riding a bicycle. He really could do marvellous things with his lean, wiry body! 'There will be a whole week between the end of this show and the beginning of the next, Jimmy. Quite a holiday!'

'Oh, what fun!' cried Lotta, and at once began to plan picnics and walks with Jimmy. 'I shan't be sorry to say goodbye to that horrid Fric!'

Before the tents were taken down, and before the caravans were made ready to leave Greenville, the tigers left in their great travelling-box. Jimmy had asked Roma's permission to say goodbye to each of them, before they left, and he was sad when he went into their cages for the last time.

He had left Lucky in his caravan, for Lucky was frightened of the tigers, and would not come near their cages if she could help it. Lotta and Mrs Brown were doing some washing down by the stream. Brownie was helping to pack up the cage that the tigers used in the ring.

'Goodbye, Queenie; goodbye, Ruby,' said the little boy, rubbing the great tigers' heads as they purred deafeningly into his ear. 'Goodbye, Busuka; don't forget me! Remember me when you are far away, for some day I will see you all again. Goodbye, all of you!'

There was a shout from outside. Everything was ready. Jimmy slipped out of the cage, and Roma came to lock the travelling-box carefully and shut up the open side so that the tigers could not be disturbed by anything they saw whilst on the road.

'Where's Fric?' said Jimmy. 'I must say goodbye to him.'

'I saw him over by your caravan just now,' said Roma. Tell him to come at once. I'm ready.'

But there was no Fric by Jimmy's caravan, and Jimmy ran back to Roma, who was just driving the heavy travelling-cage through the field-gate.

'I can't see Fric!' he called.

'He's just got in at the back!' shouted Roma. 'Goodbye!'

Fric did not peep out to wave goodbye. There was no sign of him. The engine of the powerful motor-van roared, and the tigers roared too. Down the road they went, very slowly—they were gone!

Jimmy stared after them. Goodbye to the tigers— but it would soon be welcome to the bears! How exciting it was to belong to a circus! You simply never knew what was going to come next!

He went over to Sticky Stanley and watched him practising running on his hands. Jimmy could still not walk properly on his hands. He watched Stanley turning quick somersaults, head-over-heels, heels-over-head, head-over-heels, so quickly that the little boy could hardly follow him!

'Lucky might be able to learn that!' thought Jimmy. 'I believe she could. I'll get her and make her watch old Stanley.'

He ran to his caravan and opened the door. He whistled softly. 'Lucky!' he called. 'Come along!'

But Lucky did not leap out of the door as she usually did. Only Lulu, the black spaniel, put up her sleepy head and wagged a lazy tail.

'Lucky!' called Jimmy sharply, looking quickly round the caravan. 'Lucky!'

But Lucky was not in the caravan. Jimmy ran to Mrs Brown and Lotta, who were still by the stream.

'Have you got Lucky?' he asked.

'No,' said Lotta. 'You shut her in the caravan.'

'Well, she's not there now,' said Jimmy. 'Haven't you seen her anywhere about?'

'No,' said Mrs Brown and Lotta. We've been busy.'

'She's somewhere about, I expect,' said Mrs Brown. Dogs usually are!'

Jimmy ran off. He hunted all round the circus. He asked everyone he met if they had seen Lucky. He looked under every caravan. He ran down the road

Goodbye to the Tigers

But there was no sign of Lucky at all.

and up. But there was no sign of Lucky at all. It was very strange and very worrying.

'Now, boy, now!' said Mr Galliano, when he saw Jimmy crawling out from under his caravan. 'What are you doing there? Do you want to see how many wheels my caravan has—yes?'

But Jimmy could not smile. 'No, sir,' he said. 'I'm looking for Lucky. She's disappeared!'

'A dog cannot disappear, no!' said Mr Galliano. 'She will turn up when it is her dinnertime, yes. That is the way of all animals—little boys too!'

So Jimmy waited and watched until it was Lucky's meal-time—but no Lucky came running up, hungry and eager. Lotta was worried too, and even Mrs Brown looked puzzled.

'I don't see how Lucky can disappear all at once like this,' she said. 'You don't think, Jimmy, that she has been stolen?'

'Oh, Mother, don't say that!' cried poor Jimmy, his heart sinking. 'Lucky, little dog Lucky, wherever can you be?'

Where Can Lucky Be?

Could Lucky really have been stolen? But who would have stolen her? There had been no strangers round the camp at all. Jimmy was almost in despair as he ran to and fro, begging for news of Lucky.

Lotta was crying. She loved Lucky, and she could not bear to see Jimmy's white, anxious face. What would Jimmy do if he could not find Lucky? He would not be able to go into the ring any more!

'It's a good thing we have a week between the end of this show and the beginning of the next,' thought the little girl, scrubbing her face dry as she saw Jimmy coming. 'Any news, Jimmy?'

'No,' said Jimmy. 'I've asked everybody, but nobody has seen Lucky.'

'Look, there is Lilliput beckoning to you,' said Lotta. Jimmy turned and saw Lilliput waving, and Jemima was beckoning, too, with her tiny finger!

Jimmy went across to Lilliput's caravan. Lilliput looked grave.

'I've been thinking, Jimmy,' he began, 'and I believe I know who has taken Lucky—if she has been stolen.'

'Who?' asked Jimmy.

'Fric!' said Lilliput. 'I remember now seeing him coming from your caravan, and he had a bag in his hand and the bag was wriggling!'

'What! Do you suppose he had poor little Lucky inside the bag?' cried Jimmy, a great rage creeping over him.

'Yes,' said Lilliput. 'And what's more, if the tigers hadn't been bellowing so, and the motor-van making such a noise, I guess I'd have heard whines coming from that bag, too!'

'Oh, Lilliput, I believe you are right,' said Jimmy, in despair. 'Fric was furious with Lotta and with me because he got a scolding from Roma—and he knew Lucky was worth a lot of money. What would he do with her?'

'Sell her, I expect,' said Lilliput. 'But it's up to us to get her back before he does. We'll go after Roma and Fric!'

'But I don't know where they've gone!' cried Jimmy.

'We can find out from Galliano,' said Lilliput. 'I'll come with you, Jimmy. You saved Jemima for me, when she was in the tigers' cage, and I told you I'd help you if ever you needed help.'

'I didn't think I'd need it so soon,' said Jimmy sadly. 'You're a good friend, Lilliput. I wouldn't know how to follow Roma and Fric, if I had to go alone, or how to make Fric own up. You'll be a great help.'

They went to tell Mr Galliano what they meant to do. The ring-master looked as black as thunder when he heard what Lilliput had to say about Fric.

'That dog is worth a lot of money, yes!' he said. 'You must get her back somehow before the show opens at Blackpool next week, for she draws a lot of people to the circus. The tigers have gone to join Mr Briggs's circus at Five-Ways, twenty miles from here. You can get there by train. Leave tonight. I think Roma will not know anything about this, for he would not do such a wicked thing, no! Fric is stupid, and only a boy. You will see that Roma understands that Fric is to be well watched in future, Lilliput—yes? He needs a very firm hand, and he does not get it, no.'

Mr Galliano was so upset about Lucky's going that his hat was perfectly straight on his head, and he looked quite strange in it. He patted Jimmy on the shoulder and pressed some money into his hand.

There was a lump in Jimmy's throat, but he did not cry. He was too anxious even to think of tears. He and Lilliput ran to Jimmy's caravan to tell Mrs Brown, Brownie, and Lotta what they were going to do. Mrs Brown quickly put Jimmy's pyjamas into a bag, and kissed him goodbye.

'What about Jemima and the other three monkeys?' asked Lotta. 'Shall I see to them for you, Lilliput?'

'I'm taking Jemima with me,' said Lilliput. 'I've never been away from her since I had her. You see to the others for me, Lotta, there's a good girl.'

Lotta promised, and Lilliput and Jimmy said goodbye and ran to the station to get the next train to Five-Ways. They just caught it, and sat without speaking whilst it puffed along to the town of Five-Ways. Jemima had a lovely time. She got up into the luggage rack and examined everybody's bags and baskets. The other people in the carriage laughed loudly at her, but Jimmy was too sad at heart even to smile at Jemima's funny ways.

Lilliput had to put her under his coat at last because she tried to pick the flowers out of a lady's hat. The monkey chattered a little and then went to sleep.

They got out at Five-Ways, which was a big station. Lilliput asked the porter where Mr Briggs's circus was. 'Go down that street, keep up over the hill and make for the Common,' said the porter. 'The circus is camping in the big field at the beginning of the Common. Take a tram. It's a long way.'

So the two took a tram, and went through many dingy streets until at last they had a sight of the Common—and there, in a great field, was Mr Briggs's circus, with tents, caravans, and cages, just as Mr Galliano's had.

'Now you leave this to me, Jimmy,' said Lilliput, as they went in at the gate and made their way to the big travelling-box of tigers they knew so well. 'There's Roma, look! Hi, Roma!'

Roma turned, and stared in the greatest astonishment at Lilliput and Jimmy.

'Have *you* come to join the circus too?' he cried. 'I'm glad to see you. Hello, Jemima! Got over your adventure yet?'

'I want to see Fric,' said Lilliput in a grave voice.

'Why?' asked Roma at once. 'What has he done, the young scamp?'

'Roma, Jimmy's dog Lucky has disappeared,' said Lilliput. 'I saw Fric coming from the direction of Jimmy's caravan, carrying a bag—and we have an idea that he knows something about Lucky.'

'The bad boy! The tiresome lad!' cried Roma, who often had reason to find fault with Fric. 'But I

91

haven't seen anything of Lucky on our journey here, Lilliput. Are you sure that Lucky hasn't run off somewhere, meaning to come back tonight?'

'Lucky never runs far from me,' said Jimmy. 'Where is Fric, Roma? Call him.'

'He has gone shopping into the town,' said Roma.

'Did he take a bag with him?' asked Lilliput quickly.

'I didn't see him go,' said Roma. 'Wait here for a little, and he will be back. I am going to have my supper. Will you have some too?'

Lilliput was hungry, and he sat down to share Roma's sausages, but Jimmy felt sick and could eat nothing. He sat waiting for Fric to come back. At last he saw him coming in at the gate, carrying a bag full of something. Jimmy flew over the field at once.

'What's in that bag, Fric?' he shouted. 'Give it to me!'

Fric looked astonished and frightened. 'Hello,' he said. 'This *is* a surprise. What are you here for?'

'I guess you know all right,' said Jimmy, in a fierce voice. 'Give me that bag!'

Fric threw it to him with a laugh. Jimmy opened it with trembling hands. Inside there were potatoes and two tins of pineapple chunks. Nothing else. Jimmy dropped the bag on the ground and faced Fric.

'What have you done with Lucky?' he demanded.

'Lucky! Whatever are you talking about!' said Fric, a surprised look on his face. Just then Lilliput and Roma came up. Roma took Fric by the shoulder and spoke to him sternly.

'Fric, you will say truly whether you took Lucky or not, and what you have done with her? Come now, speak up.'

'I don't know anything about Lucky,' said Fric sulkily, and not another thing could any of the three get out of him. He would say nothing but that. Lilliput looked at Jimmy in despair. None of them believed Fric, but if he chose to say nothing, what could they do? They had no real proof that he had taken the little dog away.

'Turn out your pockets, Fric,' said Roma suddenly.

'No,' said Fric. 'Why should I?'

'Did you hear what I said?' roared Roma. Fric sullenly turned out his pockets, and in them was quite a lot of money!

'How did you get that?' demanded Roma at once.

'It's my savings,' said Fric, putting the notes back into his pocket. 'Can't I have savings?'

'You've sold Lucky to someone!' shouted Jimmy, and he shook Fric till his teeth rattled in his head. 'You've sold my little dog!'

'I haven't!' cried Fric. 'Let me go!'

Just then Mr Briggs, the owner of the circus, came up. He stared at Jimmy and Lilliput and then flipped a thumb towards the gate.

'Out!' he said. 'You don't belong here!'

There was nothing more that Lilliput and Jimmy could do. Carrying the frightened Jemima, Lilliput and the little boy went towards the field-gate, Jimmy white with anger, for he felt perfectly certain that Fric had sold Lucky to somebody in the big town.

'What can we do now, Lilliput?' Jimmy said, in a trembling voice.

'We'll take lodgings somewhere for the night,' said Lilliput, putting his arm comfortingly round the little boy. 'Tomorrow morning we will go to old Ma Lightfoot. She knows all the circus folk, and she'll be able to tell us who that spiteful Fric might have gone to with Lucky. Don't worry now, Jimmy; Lucky will be all right. Whoever has bought her will take great care of her, for she's valuable. I reckon they hope to sell her to another circus, when they see the chance.'

They looked for lodgings, and at last found a clean little house in a dirty street. The woman who took them in didn't mind Jemima a bit. She said she had once had a man lodging with her who had two

'What have you done with Lucky?'

young bears—and after that, well, she didn't mind anything!

'You must have something to eat, Jimmy,' said Lilliput. 'I'll get the woman to bring up a meal.'

So a lovely stew was sent up for the two of them, and although Jimmy felt sure he wouldn't be able to eat any of it, because he was so worried, he found that he could—and felt much better after it!

Lilliput was the best of friends to Jimmy that night. He wouldn't let the little boy think and worry, but told him such lovely tales of circus life that Jimmy simply had to listen! When they said goodnight, Jemima crept in beside Jimmy and snuggled down.

'Cheer up, Jimmy,' said Lilliput. 'We'll get Lucky soon, never fear!'

Lotta Disappears

The next morning Jimmy awoke early and lay thinking about Lucky. Where was she? Was she missing him? Did she wonder why her little master was not with her to pet her and feed her? For the first time tears came into Jimmy's eyes and he sniffed so loudly that Lilliput awoke. Jemima heard the sniff too, and awoke. She wriggled out of Jimmy's bed, sat on the bed-rail and chattered at them. She looked so comical that Jimmy had to smile.

'Breakfast!' said Lilliput, smelling a good smell of bacon frying. 'Come on, Jimmy!'

After breakfast the two, with Jemima, set out to find Ma Lightfoot. She lived in a tiny house, with three parrots, two monkeys, one fox cub, three cats, and four dogs. Jimmy could hardly hear himself speak, because the parrots made so much noise. Jemima shrieked with joy when she saw the two monkeys in their cage, and at once sat on the top and chattered to them.

Ma Lightfoot was a very kindly woman, with light, piercing eyes and big gentle hands. She had been in a circus when she was young, and had trained many animals. Now she kept animals for those who wanted to board them out for a while, so hers was always an exciting house to go to. You never knew if you were going to meet a young bear in the shed, or tame white rats all over the place!

Lilliput told Ma Lightfoot all about Jimmy and Lucky, and she nodded her head.

'Yes,' she said. 'I have heard of this boy and his clever dog. He has the same gift as I have—he understands and loves, and so all animals and birds are his friends. Be quiet, Polly. Be quiet, Sally!'

The parrots stopped screeching, and one tried to catch Jemima's tail. Jemima threw a handful of seed at her. She screeched again, and the third one said, very solemnly, 'Pop goes the weasel!'

When the animals and birds had quietened down once more, and Jimmy had removed the fox cub from his knee, where it would keep biting off his coat buttons, Lilliput asked Ma Lightfoot what he wanted to know.

'Is there anyone in this town who would buy a stolen animal, meaning to resell it when he had a chance?' said Lilliput. Ma Lightfoot nodded her head.

'Yes,' she said. 'There's Charlie Tipps. You've heard of him, I dare say. He was turned out of all the circuses for stealing. Never could keep his hands off other people's belongings. He'd buy Lucky, hide her away, and sell her to another circus when he got the chance. You'd better go and see him. Maybe you could frighten him, and he'd give you back Lucky.'

Jimmy wanted to be off at once, so the boy, the man, and the monkey set off to the address Ma Lightfoot had given them. Jimmy was full of ideas. He was quite sure that Charlie Tipps had bought Lucky, and would be hiding her somewhere in the house.

'I shall shout "Lucky! Lucky! Lucky!" at the top of my voice as soon as the door is opened!' he said. 'And I shall whistle too—and if Lucky is anywhere about she'll answer me by barking, even if she can't get to me. And whilst you argue with Charlie, I shall slip off and look into every room of the house, Lilliput.'

'Right,' said Lilliput. 'We ought to find her if she's there!'

They came to the house. It stood by itself in a lonely street. There was a big garden with sheds here and there, for Charlie often kept animals of different sorts, and sold or exchanged them to circuses and fairs. Jimmy was certain Lucky was somewhere about.

They banged on the big knocker. Clang, clang, clang! They rang the bell too. A woman opened the door, looking surprised at all the noise. She looked even more surprised when Jimmy pushed by her, yelling 'Lucky! Lucky! Lucky!' and whistled piercingly in her ear.

'Where's Charlie Tipps?' demanded Lilliput, putting on his fiercest expression.

'He's not here,' said the woman. 'He went off early this morning in his car. I don't know where he's gone. He won't be back for two weeks. He's taken a load of animals to sell to some circuses.'

Jimmy's heart sank. Lucky must have been taken too! He rushed into every room; he went into the garden and looked into every shed. He shouted and whistled, but no little dog answered him. The boy went back to Lilliput, bitterly disappointed.

'We can't do any more here,' said Lilliput, sad to see Jimmy's unhappy face. 'Come along. We'd best go back to the circus. Our luck's right out.'

The woman banged the door after them, angry with the boy who had rushed through the house, shouting and whistling. Lilliput and Jimmy walked back to the station, not saying a word.

Everyone at Galliano's circus was sorry for Jimmy. They all loved animals and they knew what it was to give one's heart to any creature, and then to lose it. Mr Wally patted Jimmy on the back. Mr Tonks didn't know what to say, so he just shook hands. Even Mr Galliano was more upset than anyone had ever seen him, for he was proud of Lucky and very fond of Jimmy. Lotta slipped her arms round Jimmy—but to her surprise and dismay Jimmy pushed her away. 'I only want to tell you I'm sorry, Jimmy,' she said, very much hurt.

'If you hadn't gone spying on me that night I went to the tigers' cage, and got us all into that trouble over Jemima, Fric would never have tried to pay me out by stealing little dog Lucky,' said Jimmy. 'It's all your fault!'

'Oh, Jimmy, that's not fair!' said poor Lotta, bursting into tears. But Jimmy was past being fair or kind. He was so anxious, so disappointed, and so unhappy that he just didn't care what he said or did to Lotta. His mother heard all that was said, and was sorry for both children. She called them.

'Come and have your dinner. I've something extra-special.'

But the extra-special dinner wasn't eaten. Lotta ran away to cry by herself, and Jimmy wouldn't stir from his seat on an upturned tub. He seemed to be quite a changed boy. But Brownie, his father, soon pulled him together.

'This is not the way to meet trouble, Jimmy,' he said sternly. 'The world hasn't come to an end because you have lost Lucky. Go up into the caravan and have your dinner. And don't blame others for what has been as much your fault! You know that it was wrong to borrow Roma's keys without his knowing.'

Jimmy obeyed has father, but he could not eat any dinner, he could only drink the coffee his mother had made. Lotta did not appear at all. Mr Tonks called to Jimmy to help him with Jumbo afterwards, and he managed to keep the little boy really busy until it was time for bed.

By that time Jimmy was very sorry that he had spoken so unfairly to Lotta. He knew he had been very unkind. He called to his mother.

'Where's Lotta, do you know?'

'I haven't seen her since dinner time,' said Mrs Brown. 'She didn't come in to tea. I thought perhaps you two had made up your silly quarrel, and she was with you.'

'No, I haven't seen her,' said Jimmy. 'I'll go and find her.'

But he couldn't find her, and at last he went back to the caravan. 'Has Lotta come in?' he asked. 'Is supper ready? I do feel hungry.'

'I should think you do!' said Mrs Brown. 'No dinner, and no tea! I've got a nice supper for you. Lotta hasn't come back. She'll be in sometime. Maybe she's gone for a walk with Lulu.'

'Oh, if she's taken Lulu, then she's certainly gone for a walk,' said Jimmy, and he went up the steps, sniffing at the good supper Mrs Brown had cooked

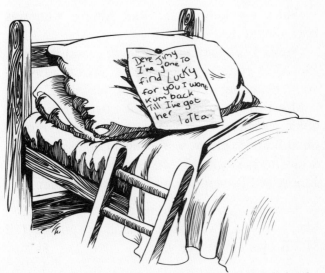

Pinned onto Jimmy's pillow was a note in Lotta's babyish handwriting.

for him. He thought of Lucky with a pain at his heart. What was Lucky doing now? Where was she? Would she run away and come back to him? She was quite clever enough!

The Browns ate their supper. It was dark now, and still Lotta hadn't come back. Mr Brown began to get worried.

'She ought to be back now,' he said. 'I wish I knew where she had gone and I'd go and meet her. She's in our charge, and I don't like her out as late as this, all alone.'

'She's got Lulu, Dad,' said Jimmy, who was beginning to feel worried.

'Well, I'm glad to hear *that*,' said Brownie. 'She'll be company for Lotta, at any rate. Jimmy, you'd better get to bed. You look very tired.'

Mrs Brown turned back the cover of Jimmy's bunk, and then she gave a cry of surprise. Pinned on to Jimmy's pillow was a note in Lotta's babyish, scrawling handwriting. Mrs Brown picked it up, and Jimmy and Brownie stood beside her, reading it.

'Dere Jimmy,' said the note, 'I've gone to find Lucky for you. I wont kum back till I've got her. Tell Mrs Brown not to wurry.

Lotta.'

'Good gracious!' said Mrs Brown at once. 'Whatever does the child mean? How can she find Lucky, any more than Jimmy or Lilliput could? Wherever has she gone? Oh dear, dear, what a worry—as if we hadn't enough without Lotta disappearing too!'

Jimmy was horrified. Lotta going off all by herself with Lulu to find Lucky, when she had no idea at all where the little dog could be! What would she do? Oh dear, this was even worse than Lucky's disappearance!

Off went Brownie to tell Mr Galliano. Soon everyone knew, and there was a great chattering and wakefulness in the camp. Lotta! Where was she? Nobody had seen her go. Nobody had seen Lulu. Nobody knew what to do.

And where was Lotta all this time? Ah, Jimmy would have been surprised if he had known!

Lotta's Amazing Adventure

Lotta had felt very unhappy when Jimmy had spoken to her so unkindly. She had run off crying to Lilliput's caravan, and had told the kind little monkey-man what Jimmy had said.

'Now don't fret about it,' Lilliput said, patting her on the back. 'Jimmy's dreadfully unhappy and worried himself because Lucky has been stolen. Did he tell you how we went to see Fric and Roma, and felt certain that Fric had sold Lucky to Charlie Tipps? But Charlie had gone away, we didn't know where!'

'Charlie Tipps!' said Lotta, drying her eyes. 'Why, my father, Laddo, used to know him well. He said he was a bad man, though. He once stole a white horse of ours, had it dyed black, and sold it to somebody else!'

The little girl sat thinking. If only she could get back Lucky for Jimmy! She looked at Lilliput.

'Lilliput,' she said, 'will you lend me some money?'

'Of course!' said Lilliput at once, and he took down an old brown teapot from a shelf and tipped it up. A heap of silver fell out.

'Take what you want,' said Lilliput. 'Are you needing a new dress or something?'

'No,' said Lotta, picking out some silver coins and putting them into her pocket. 'It's a secret, Lilliput. Do you mind if I don't tell you yet?'

'Not a bit,' said kindly Lilliput. 'Hey, Jemima, the money's not for you! Put that coin back!'

Jemima had stretched out a little arm and picked up a coin. She had put it inside her cheek, but Lilliput made her put it back into the teapot. 'She's artful enough to go and buy herself twelve ice-creams!' he said. 'And then she'd be ill!'

Lotta ran back to the Browns' caravan. She picked up an old raincoat and a beret. She put on a pair of shoes. Then she called softly to Lulu, the black spaniel, and together the two slipped out of the caravan, unseen by anyone.

Lotta squeezed through the hedge at the back of the caravan, and found herself on the main road. A bus was coming, and she stopped it. In she got with Lulu, and off they went together in the rumbling bus.

'I want to go to Uptown,' Lotta told the conductor. 'How near do you go to that?'

107

'Well, that's a good way away,' said the conductor in surprise. 'We only go as far as Hillocks, six miles off. But you can get a bus there to Uptown, though it will take you a long time.'

It was night before the little girl reached Uptown. She had come there because she remembered that a great friend of Charlie Tipps lived there, and her father had told her that this man was very clever at altering the appearance of animals so that they looked quite different. Then they were sold again. Lotta had an idea that Charlie Tipps might take Lucky to this man.

'Where shall I sleep?' wondered the little girl, as she and Lulu got out of the bus, feeling hungry and tired. 'I can't sleep in a house. I never have in all my life! I couldn't bear it! Come, Lulu, we'll find a place somewhere.'

Lotta bought some cakes and chocolate at a little shop, and, sharing them with Lulu, she set off out of the town towards the green hills that lay on the south.

She came to a farm. She made out the shape of a big barn in the distance, and she and Lulu went into a field, crawled through the hedge, and crept quietly to the big, shadowy barn.

She pushed the door open. In the barn were stacked sacks full of something soft. 'These will do nicely for a bed, Lulu,' said Lotta. The little girl pulled some into a nice soft heap and lay down. She was very tired. She threw the old raincoat over her, and pulled Lulu close to her.

'I'm lonely, Lulu,' she whispered. 'I'll hug you, and we'll keep each other nice and warm.'

Lulu licked Lotta's nose. She was a gentle, loving dog, and it was a great comfort to Lotta to have her for company. Soon the two were fast asleep.

In the morning Lotta washed her face in a nearby stream. She did not brush or comb her hair, for she had brought neither brush nor comb with her. She shook her mop of black curls just as Lulu shook her silky black ears and coat! Then they set off back to Uptown.

'We've got to find Mr Binks, Charlie's friend,' she told Lulu, 'That was his name, I remember. But we mustn't let him see us, Lulu, for he might remember me. I went with Lal and Laddo when they went to see him about our white horse that was stolen. We must be very careful.'

Lotta asked at a post office for Mr Binks's address, for she had forgotten it. There were three Mr Binks living in the town, but as soon as she heard the address of the second one, the little girl remembered. That was the one!

She set off to find it, munching bread and chocolate. Lulu had made a good meal of some fresh meat at a butcher's. She trotted along happily by Lotta's feet, wondering what all the adventure was about.

At last Lotta came to a low, rambling farmhouse, which she remembered from two or three years before. There were big stables in the fields beyond, and many sheds and kennels. Lotta stood behind the hedge and gazed in. Was Lucky there? How she longed to know! But there were so many dogs barking, so many horses neighing, so many hens clucking, that it was impossible to hear if Lucky's sharp bark was among them! She watched horses being ridden round a large field. They were being trained for a circus, and they were most beautifully kept. Lotta wished she could ride one!

Suddenly an idea flashed into the little girl's head. If she dressed up as a boy, nobody would know her! She could go into the fields there, and even if Mr Binks saw her he would not remember her. She turned and ran back to the shops.

She went into a hairdresser's, and asked for all her pretty black curls to be cut short, like a boy's. The girl did not want to do it, but Lotta suddenly took a pair of scissors and began to chop off her curls herself, so the hairdresser had to finish the job properly. What a funny little thing Lotta looked when she came out!

Then she bought a shirt and a pair of blue shorts at another shop. She slipped behind a hedge on her way back to Mr Binks's house, and changed into her new clothes. When she came through the hedge into the road again, she looked exactly like a little boy!

Lotta felt rather grand. She stuck her hands into her pockets, and whistled as she went, with Lulu at her heels. The spaniel did not seem to notice that Lotta was any different. She smelt the same, and that was all that Lulu cared about!

And now Lotta went boldly into the fields around the farmhouse and examined every shed and stable to see if little dog Lucky was there. But she could not find any sign of her. 'She must be in the farmhouse somewhere,' thought Lotta.

And then a most extraordinary thing happened. A big car drew up outside the farmhouse, and out got Mr Alfred Cyrano, head of one of the biggest circuses, a man who had once offered to buy Lucky from Jimmy! Lotta knew him at once, and she stared in amazement.

Her quick little brain set to work at once. 'He always wanted Lucky, and everyone knew it! Oh, he must have come for Lucky! So Lucky is here!

He'll take her away with him. If only I could go with him! But how?'

Mr Alfred Cyrano went into the farmhouse. Lotta crept round, trying to see into the windows. At last she discovered that Cyrano and Mr Binks were at the back of the house, overlooking the fields where the horses were cantering. On the floor was a small travelling-box, big enough for a dog.

For a moment Lotta did not know what to do. Then the sound of the cantering of hoofs put an idea into her head. She would do some tricks on those horses, hoping that the two men would look out of the window and see her! Then maybe she could beg a job from Mr Cyrano, and go with him back to his circus—with Lucky! And if she didn't manage to escape somehow on the way, taking Lucky with her, she wouldn't be as clever as she thought she was!

The little girl's heart began to beat fast. She ran to a great black horse with a broad back. He had no saddle and no bridle. He shied away as Lotta came up. But the little girl swung herself up on to his back and galloped him round the field, whilst two men who were exercising the horses shouted angrily at her!

Lotta knelt on the galloping horse. She stood up! She stretched out her arms, and there she was, going lightly up and down on the galloping horse, waving to the two astonished grooms as she passed them.

From the corner of her eye she saw that Mr Binks and Mr Cyrano, hearing the shouts, had come to the window and were staring in amazement. The little girl dropped down to the horse's back, got up again, and this time stood facing backwards, looking over the horse's tail. Then she stood first on one leg and then on the other! She jumped up and down! It was marvellous!

Lotta had been a circus girl all her life, but the horse she was on was only half trained, and a stranger to her. He began to gallop so fast that Lotta had to sit down again. One of the grooms was afraid the boy—as he thought Lotta was—would be hurt. He galloped up on another horse, shouting to Lotta to let him drag her off.

But the little girl stood up again, and when the groom's horse came alongside she neatly jumped on to his own horse, just behind him, and stood there, her hand lightly on his shoulder. He brought his horse to a stop. But before he could speak to her, a loud voice shouted from the farmhouse:

'Come here, you! Who are you?'

It was Mr Cyrano, who had been watching Lotta's performance in astonishment. Lotta jumped from the groom's horse and ran up to him in her shirt and shorts.

'Who are you?' asked Cyrano again. Lotta decided to be grand.

'I am the Boy Wonder!' she said. 'Barney Beano, the Boy Wonder! I can ride any horse in the world! I'm looking for a job.'

'Well, you can ride, that's certain,' said Mr Cyrano. 'Got any luggage? You can come back with me now, if you like, and start next week.'

'I've got no luggage,' said Lotta, 'but I've got a dog. Can I bring her?'

'Yes,' said Cyrano, and he turned to go inside the house with Mr Binks. Lotta whistled to Lulu, and the two went and waited by the gate. Soon Mr Binks came to the door and beckoned. 'Take this box to the car for Mr Cyrano,' he ordered.

Lotta flew to get the box. Could Lucky be inside it? There was no sound inside, and Lotta did not dare even to whisper Lucky's name. But Lulu seemed strangely excited at the box, and sniffed all round it when it was in the car.

Mr Cyrano got in and took the wheel. Lotta was at the back with Lulu and the dog-box. Mr Binks called goodbye and the car slid down the lane.

The Boy Wonder was off to Mr Alfred Cyrano's circus! How Lotta wished that Jimmy could see where she was now!

114

Little Dog Lucky!

Mr Cyrano's circus was a long way away. It was three hours before they arrived there, and Lotta was very hungry. The dog in the travelling-box had not made a sound, and even though Lotta had whispered Lucky's name, no answering whine or bark had come. It was puzzling.

When they arrived at the circus, Mr Cyrano bellowed for a man called Tiny. Tiny was simply enormous, so it made people laugh when they heard his name.

He came up. Mr Cyrano waved him to the back of the car. 'You'll find the dog I told you about in a box there,' he said. 'He's been given some sleep-medicine, so he'll have to sleep it off. He'll be all right tomorrow. Take this boy too and let him have a bunk in your caravan. He'll help with the horses and ride in the ring next week.'

Lotta went off with Tiny, who seemed quite friendly. Lulu followed at her heels. Tiny cut Lotta some bread-and-cheese sandwiches, and read the paper whilst Lotta and Lulu ate them. And then, quite suddenly, Lotta saw her own picture looking at her from the paper. What a shock she got!

She read what was printed underneath. It said: 'LOTTA, THE MISSING CIRCUS GIRL. MR AND MRS BROWN ARE VERY WORRIED ABOUT HER, BECAUSE THEY ARE IN CHARGE OF HER WHILST HER PARENTS ARE ABROAD. A REWARD IS OFFERED TO ANYONE WHO WILL BRING HER BACK.'

How glad Lotta was that she had dressed up as a boy! Nobody would know her—and she couldn't, couldn't go back till she had got little dog Lucky again! What a good thing nothing was said in the paper about Lulu!

Tiny had placed the dog-box inside an empty cage, which had its side up, so that Lotta could not see inside. So the little girl had not been able to find out if Lucky was in the box or not. She made up her mind to slip out of the caravan that night and find out. She noticed that Tiny put his cage-keys on a little shelf.

So when the camp was in darkness, and Tiny was snoring in the caravan, Lotta picked up a torch from the shelf, took the keys gently, and stole down the steps with Lulu like a black shadow. She made her way to the cage nearby and unlocked it. A little whine greeted her. Lucky had evidently awakened!

The little girl shut the door behind her, and flashed her torch in front of her, longing to see little dog Lucky, with her half-brown, half-black head, and her black spot and brown spot on her white back.

But quite a different dog looked up at her with wagging tail and friendly yelps! Lotta stared in surprise and dismay! Tears came into her eyes. Surely she hadn't gone so far in this adventure for a strange dog! Lulu ran up to the dog and sniffed her happily.

'Your head is quite black, not brown and black!' said Lotta. 'And your tail is black too. Lucky's was white! And you've got four black spots on your back instead of one brown and one black!'

The little dog jumped up at Lotta, licked her and pawed her gladly. 'You do look so like Lucky, and you act just like Lucky!' said Lotta. 'I wonder, oh, I wonder if they've dyed your dear little head and the spots on your coat and your tail to make you different! Are you Lucky?'

'Woof!' said the little dog, and she got up on her hind legs and began to do some of the tricks that Jimmy and Lotta had taught her.

Then the little girl knew for certain that it was little dog Lucky, altered so that no one should know her. She was to be trained for Mr Cyrano's circus, and he would make a lot of money! Perhaps he didn't know—perhaps Mr Binks had made Lucky different and sold her to Mr Cyrano simply as a very clever dog, easy to train. Lotta didn't care. All she knew was that she had got Lucky back—and she was going to take her to Jimmy as soon as ever she could!

'Yes—and we'll start this very minute!' said the little girl, excited. 'Come, Lucky! Come, Lulu!'

The three slipped out of the cage and set off for the gate. It was shut. Lotta climbed over it and the dogs squeezed under. Lotta did not know which way to go, but she was quite determined to put as much road between her and Mr Cyrano's circus as she could!

For hours the three of them tramped down dark roads till Lotta was almost dropping with sleep. She found an old haystack and pulled out some hay to make a bed. She lay down against the stack with the two dogs, and slept till the sun was high in the sky!

Now she had to find out where she was. She asked at a farmhouse and found that she was at a place she had never heard of. 'I want to go to Greenville,' said Lotta. 'Is there a train that goes there?'

The farmer looked at the dirty, untidy little boy with two dogs. What a little ragamuffin he looked!

'You walk to the station and ask,' he said. 'I've never heard of Greenville!'

So off went Lotta again, asking the way to the station and on the way a car passed her. Who do you suppose was driving it? Mr Alfred Cyrano, looking very angry indeed, for he had heard that the Boy Wonder had run off in the night with the valuable dog he had just bought!

And Mr Cyrano saw Lotta walking along the road with the two dogs! He stopped the car and ran back, shouting angrily. But was Lotta afraid of him? Not a bit.

'If you come any nearer my dogs will bite you!' said the little girl. 'So be careful! Show your teeth, Lulu; show yours, Lucky!'

Both dogs bared their teeth and snarled at Mr Cyrano. Then, as quick as lightning, the little girl ran to the hedge and squeezed through it, running across the fields like a hare, the two dogs beside her. Mr Cyrano knew he would never catch them.

Lotta reached the station at last. It was quite a big one and the little girl bought sandwiches and milk for herself and the two hungry dogs. Then she sat down to wait for the train to come. She was very happy. What would Jimmy say when she walked into the camp with Lucky? He would forgive her, she was sure, for anything she had done that he might blame her for.

Jimmy and Mrs Brown were very worried, for they loved Lotta and were afraid something might happen to her, going off alone with only Lulu for company. Poor Jimmy was more worried than anyone, for he felt it was his fault that Lotta had gone—and he kept thinking first of his lost dog Lucky, then of Lotta, then of Lucky, and he felt very lonely indeed without either of his best friends.

Towards the evening of the second day that Lotta had been gone, Jimmy looked out of his caravan. He saw a strange little figure coming in at the circus gate.

'Look at that boy, Mother,' said Jimmy. 'I wonder who he is—oh, Mother, Lulu's with him! Do you think he knows anything about Lotta?'

'There's another dog too,' said his mother, as Lucky came bounding through the gate, delighted to be back in her own camp again. There was a shriek from Jimmy.

'Mother! It's Lucky—my own Lucky!'

'No, it isn't,' said Mrs Brown. 'It's not a bit like Lucky!' But Jimmy would have known Lucky if she had been painted blue and yellow and red! No matter whether her head was a different colour and her spots changed, he would know his little dog a mile away! He leapt off the caravan steps and tore to the gate, yelling 'Lucky! Lucky! Lucky!'

Lucky yelped back in excitement and ran to meet her little master. She sprang straight into his arms and lay there, licking his face as fast as she could. Jimmy hugged her and cried, and cried and hugged her, and everyone came running up to see what was happening.

He leapt off the caravan steps and tore to the gate.

Jimmy looked up at last, and saw the strange little boy nearby, watching with a delighted grin. Jimmy stared and stared—this boy was so like Lotta; did Lotta have a brother?—could it possibly *be* Lotta?

Then the little girl made one of her dreadful faces and gave Jimmy a pinch—ah, it was Lotta all right!

'Lotta!' shouted Jimmy, and hugged her as well as he could with Lucky still in his arms. 'Lotta! You darling! You've got Lucky back. But why is your hair short? Why are you dressed like that? Where have you been? Why ...'

Lotta laughed joyfully. She took hold of Jimmy's arm. 'I've had such an adventure!' she said. 'But I'm so hungry. Let's go into the caravan and have supper, and I'll tell you everything!'

Mr Galliano came hurrying up at that moment. He lifted Lotta up on to his shoulder and patted little dog Lucky in delight.

'And here is Lotta come back as a boy!' he shouted, his hat very much on one side. 'And here is Lucky come back as another dog, yes! You will come and have supper with me in my caravan and tell me all your news, Lotta!'

This was a great honour. Mr Brown, Mrs Brown, Lotta, Jimmy, and the two dogs all crowded into Mr Galliano's big caravan to eat a fine supper that Mrs

Galliano cooked. Mrs Brown wanted Lotta to wash her hands and face, but the little girl wouldn't.

'Not just this once, please,' she begged. 'I can't wait to tell you all my adventures, Mrs Brown!'

So over a delicious supper of fried sausages, potatoes in their skins, fruit salad and cream, Lotta told her story, whilst Lucky sat on Jimmy's knee, licking Jimmy's hand whenever he raised it to his mouth.

The little girl was almost asleep as she finished her tale. Brownie carried her back to their caravan, and Jimmy and the dogs and his mother went too.

Jimmy was very happy now. He had got back Lucky, and Mr Galliano had told him that he had only to give the little dog a special kind of bath to get him back to his right colour—and he had got Lotta back safely too.

'Lotta, are you asleep?' whispered Jimmy. 'I just want to say I'm sorry for the unkind things I said to you. They weren't true and I didn't mean them. You're the finest girl in the world!'

'It's all right, Jimmy,' said Lotta sleepily. 'I don't mind a bit now that everything's all right! See you tomorrow!' And she fell fast asleep. But Jimmy lay awake a long, long time, planning how to reward Lotta for getting back his precious dog Lucky again. What would she like best in all the world?

Lotta Gets a Fine Reward

When Lotta awoke the next morning she was very happy. She lay in her bunk, warm and cosy, thinking of all the adventures she had had that week. She saw the golden sunshine coming in through the eastern caravan window, and she sat up.

'Jimmy!' she whispered. 'Wake up! It's very early, and it's a lovely day. Let's take Lucky and Lulu for a walk!'

Jimmy awoke. His first thought was for Lucky. He had got Lucky back again! He put out his hand and felt the little dog who was lying on his feet. But what a strange Lucky she seemed, with her altered colouring! Never mind—she should have a special bath that day and wash off all the dye that had been rubbed into her silky coat.

'Come on, Jimmy!' said Lotta. So the two of them quickly dressed and opened the caravan door very quietly. The dogs leapt down after them.

'Oh, Jimmy, I do feel happy now!' cried Lotta. 'Down, Lucky! Down, Lulu! They're happy too,

Jimmy. Oh, I was so miserable when Fric was here, and I was so afraid you'd get hurt going in the tigers' cage alone.'

'Let's forget it all,' said Jimmy, racing in front. 'I loved the tigers, but when I think of Fric and how unkind he was to Jemima and to Lucky, I feel as if I hate him. My mother says it's best not to hate anyone, because you poison your own mind if you do, so I'm going to forget all about it!'

'Good idea!' said Lotta, laughing. 'Oh, what a lovely morning, Jimmy! Look at the blue sky—and those high white clouds like cotton-wool—and look at the buttercups all over the place like a carpet of gold!'

'Lotta,' said Jimmy, suddenly standing still and taking hold of one of her hands, 'I want to give you a reward for saving Lucky, but I can't think what to give you. Tell me something. Is there anything you want?'

'Nothing,' said Lotta. 'At least, there's only one thing I want, and that is to have Lal and Laddo back again, so that I can ride a horse in the ring once more. I miss my father and mother, though yours are very sweet to me, Jimmy. But I do long for a horse of my own to ride again.'

'I'll buy you one!' cried Jimmy. 'I've heaps and heaps of money now! I was going to buy some more dogs and train them for the ring, but I'll buy you a horse instead!'

'Oh, Jimmy! Oh Jimmy!' cried Lotta, her cheeks flaming red and her eyes shining like blue forget-me-nots. 'You don't really mean it?'

'I do!' said Jimmy. 'I'll never, never forget how you ran off alone to find Lucky for me. I want to give you something for that, Lotta, though I know you don't want any reward.'

'Of course I don't want a reward,' said the little girl. 'But oh, Jimmy! A horse of my own! Where shall we get it? I'd like a little black one—a pony— that I can teach tricks to, and ride in the ring by myself! Oh, do you think Mr Galliano would let me?'

The two children were so excited about the idea that they walked for miles and came back to the camp very late for breakfast. Mrs Brown scolded them, but when she heard their new plan, she forgot about their lateness and lifted up her hands in astonishment.

'What *will* you think of next!' she cried. 'Well, Jimmy dear, your money is your own to do as you like with. You had better ask Pepita and Lou their advice. But you must hurry up, because we move from here in two days, and you won't have much holiday after that, for the next show is to be a very big one. The dancing bears are coming, you know, and they draw big crowds.'

'Hey! Is Jimmy there—yes?' called Mr Galliano's voice. 'Ah, there you are, Jimmy! Come with me and bring Lucky. Mrs Galliano has got ready his special bath, and she is waiting, yes!'

Jimmy and Lotta ran to Mrs Galliano's caravan with Lucky. Lulu followed too. A big tin bath was steaming outside Mr Galliano's caravan. It was a most peculiar colour, for the water was pale mauve with little yellow blobs floating about in it. Mrs Galliano was stirring it.

Lilliput came up to watch, with Jemima as usual round his neck. Mr Wally came up with Sammy the chimpanzee, and Tonks the elephant-man came up too. It was fun to see Lucky being bathed and brought back to her right colour again!

Sammy put his arm round Jimmy and Lotta. He loved both children. He took off his own straw hat and put it on Jimmy's head. Then he reached out to take Mr Galliano's top hat to wear himself. But Mr Wally shouted to him:

'Now, Sammy, now! You mustn't take people's hats!' So Sammy took back his own hat and tried to look good. Lucky was put into the mauve water. She didn't like it, but Mrs Galliano held her in firmly, whilst Jimmy rubbed gently. Gradually the water became black, as all the dye slid off the dog's coat. Lotta danced round in excitement.

'It's Lucky now! She looks like herself again, dear little dog! Good old Lucky!'

Lucky tried to wuff, but yelped instead, for she did hate the mauve bath. But very soon she was out of it and was being well dried, her little brown-and-black head shining in the sun. She was herself once more! Everybody cheered and clapped Lotta and Jimmy on the back. They were proud of the two children, and especially of Lotta that day, for they had all heard of her adventures.

Suddenly there was a splash. Lulu had jumped into the bath and was looking patiently up at Jimmy. 'My turn now,' her brown eyes said. She did so like to have a fuss made of her, even if she had to have a bath as well! Jimmy laughed and lifted her out.

'*Your* black won't come off, Lulu,' he said. 'Dry her, Lotta. Isn't she funny!'

Soon two excited, half-dried dogs were racing about the camp in the sunshine. Jimmy pulled Lotta's arm. 'Let's come and talk to Pepita and Lou,' he said. 'They're over there, exercising their horses. Let's go and ask them if they know of any pony that would do for you, Lotta.'

They went over to Lou, who was just dismounting from his beautiful white horse, Starshine. Juanita

Lotta Gets a Fine Reward!

Lucky was herself once more!

and Pepita were cantering round the field, leading a horse each as they went.

'Hello,' said the great big Lou, his kind face breaking into a smile. 'I am glad you have your little dog back. Lotta is a good girl—she has had a strange adventure! She dressed up as a boy and rode strange horses! She should have a horse of her own!'

'Oh, Lou, that's just what we've come to talk to you about!' said Jimmy eagerly. 'I've saved a heap of money, you know, because Lucky has earned a lot for me, and I want to buy Lotta a pony of her very own that she can train and ride!'

'So!' said Lou, nodding his big head. 'Ho there, Juanita, Pepita! Come and talk to Jimmy!'

The two young women leapt down from their black horses and came over to the children, their dark heads shining as brightly as their horses' backs. They were big and kindly, slow in their talk, and gentle with their horses.

'Jimmy wants to give Lotta a black pony to train,' said Lou. 'Has our brother such a one, little sisters?'

The two dark-eyed, dark-haired young women looked at one another and spoke quickly in a language that Jimmy could not understand. Lou nodded. He turned to the children.

'Our brother keeps horses,' he said. 'Tomorrow we go to see him. You shall go too, if you like, and see if he has a pony for Lotta.'

'We will all go,' said Pepita, in her soft, husky voice. 'Be ready at nine o'clock, children.'

Lotta rushed to tell Mrs Brown. She was so excited that she fell up the caravan steps and knocked over a tub standing just inside the caravan.

'Good gracious, Lotta, anyone would think you were an escaped bear, you are so clumsy!' said Mrs Brown with a laugh. 'Pick up the tub. What's the excitement now?'

'We're going tomorrow to buy me a pony, we're going tomorrow to buy me a pony!' yelled Lotta, catching Mrs Brown round the waist and dancing all over the caravan with her.

'Now, now, Lotta,' said Mrs Brown. 'I can't dance with a full teapot in my hand, it's dangerous!'

But Lotta was too excited to listen to anything or anyone. She longed and longed for nine o'clock next day to come!

And when at last it came, what a happy party set off to the farm up on the moors, where Lou's brother kept his beautiful horses! They rode on horseback, for most of the way was on grass and heather. Lou rode his beautiful white Starshine, a most magnificent horse with a tail that reached the ground. Pepita rode a smaller horse with a little proud head that tossed all the time. Juanita had her favourite, a gentle old horse, rather fat, but clever in all the ways of the circus.

131

The children had borrowed two of Mr Galliano's horses for the day. Lotta had a fiery one that got up on its hind legs every now and again, and made Jimmy very nervous indeed, for Jimmy was not a good horseman and never would be, though horses all loved him. He rode the safest horse in the camp, and, even so, he felt quite scared when it began to trot!

They came to the farm, and the keen moorland air blew around them, tossing the hair of Juanita and Pepita about. But poor Lotta had hair like a boy's still, though it curled tightly and would soon grow.

'Go and look at the horses whilst I see our brother,' said Lou, and he pointed to a sloping hillside where a great many horses galloped. Jimmy and Lotta rode to the hillside, and then Lotta gave a shout.

'There's the one I want!' she cried. 'Oh, Jimmy, look, there's the one I want!'

The Taming of Black Beauty

Jimmy looked to see which horse Lotta was pointing to. He saw a pony, jet-black all over, save for four white socks and a shining white star right in the middle of his black forehead. His eyes shone wickedly, and as the children looked at him he kicked up his heels and galloped away like the wind!

'Oh!' said Lotta, her face shining like the sun. 'Oh! He's the loveliest pony I've ever seen. Oh, Jimmy, dear Jimmy, do buy him for me!'

So when Lou came galloping across the fields with his brother—an even bigger, just as kindly man—the two had already made their choice.

'That's the one we want!' and Jimmy, and he pointed to the black pony. 'Is he very expensive?'

'He is a very good pony, yes,' said Lou's brother, Philip. 'But he is not for you. He is wild, so wild! No one can ride him. Already two people have bought him and sent him back because they cannot manage such a wild creature.'

'I want him,' said Lotta obstinately. 'Let me have him, please do. I'm not afraid of any horse! I can ride any horse that's got four legs!'

'Ah, but this one might have a hundred legs, he is so wild!' said Philip, smiling at the little girl. 'He bites, he kicks, he gallops like the wind. He has a wicked eye.'

'Yes, I saw that,' said Lotta. 'But he's the kind I like. Please let me have him.'

'It is impossible,' said Philip. 'Now you look at all my horses, little Miss Lotta, and you choose another. I go to speak to my sisters, for I do not see them often.'

The two big men galloped back to the farmhouse. Lotta looked sulky and her eyes gleamed as wickedly as the black pony's.

'Come, Lotta, let's choose another,' said Jimmy. 'What about that brown-and-white pony over there?'

'I want that black one,' said Lotta. 'And I'm going to get him. Jimmy, make your horse-noises.'

Jimmy laughed. He could make all kinds of animal noises, and could bring dogs to him by whining, cats to him by mewing, and other animals by making strange noises that no one, not even Lotta, could make. He began making a peculiar noise, half like a horse's whinny and half like a gramophone running down.

The horses nearby pricked up their ears. One or two cantered close. Jimmy went on. More horses came up and nuzzled his hand. Horses always adored Jimmy.

'Go on, Jimmy, go on,' whispered Lotta. 'The black pony has heard. He's coming nearer!'

So Jimmy went on making his strange noises, and gradually the horses began to talk back to him, whinnying and nuzzling round him. The black pony came close too, its ears upright, its wicked eyes watching and gleaming.

Then Lotta did a daring thing. She suddenly leapt straight from her own horse's back on to the pony's! She caught hold of its mane. In fright and anger it reared up and stood on its hind legs. But Lotta clung to its back like a limpet to a rock.

The black pony came down on all four legs, and then streaked off like the wind, galloping round the enormous field, faster than a car! Lotta bent forward and held tight. Her knees gripped the pony's back and her hands were tangled in its thick mane. Round and round the field went the pony, snorting with fear and anger.

At last, tired out, it stood still again, and Lotta began to talk to it. She had a way with horses just as Jimmy had a way with dogs. But this pony was not easy to calm or tame. In a trice it was up on its hind legs again, trying to throw Lotta off. Then it took it into its head to lie down and roll over, knowing that this was a sure way to make any rider get off.

But Lotta was waiting for this. She slipped off at once, and then, as the horse got up after rolling, the little girl leapt straight on to his back again, and off they went round the field like lightning!

Jimmy watched, open-mouthed. He had never seen such a thing before. He knew that both the pony and the little girl were trying to conquer one another. But how in the world could Lotta stay on like that with nothing to help her? She was a marvel! Only a girl brought up in the circus from babyhood could do such a thing.

Others were watching too. Lou, Philip, Pepita, and Juanita had come out to see. They said not a word, but watched gravely. Jimmy's heart beat very fast. He hoped nothing would happen to daring little Lotta. She looked like a boy on the pony, with her short hair.

At last the pony stopped. It could go no farther, could gallop no more. Foam dripped from its mouth. Its beautiful head hung down. Its legs trembled, and its eyes were dull. It was conquered.

Lotta slipped down from its back. She put her arm round its neck and stroked its soft nose. She spoke lovingly into its ear, and the tired pony listened.

Jimmy came up quietly. He spoke to the pony in his low, gentle voice, and the pony nuzzled against him.

Then Philip cantered up and called to the children, 'Take the pony to the stables and rub him down.'

'Can I have him, oh, can I have him?' called Lotta.

'You have made him yours!' answered Philip. 'We have never seen such riding, no—not in all our years in the circus. One day you will be a wonder, little girl!'

Lotta was red with excitement and delight. She led the pony away to the stables and she and Jimmy rubbed the trembling little beast down.

'I was frightened for you, Lotta,' said Jimmy.

'Well, it's tit for tat then!' said Lotta, laughing. 'I was just as frightened when you were with the tigers! Oh, Jimmy! I'm so happy. This is just the pony I've always wanted—wild, strong, beautiful, clever! Look at his eyes! You can see he'll learn anything I want to teach him!'

Jimmy knew that the pony would be clever. He, too, liked the wilful, independent little thing, and he thought secretly that the pony was rather like Lotta herself, wild and daring and clever! He was very glad that the little girl had the one she wanted.

'I shall ride him home,' said Lotta. 'He will be fresh again by the time we've had our dinner. What shall we call him?'

Jimmy looked at the pony with its sleek black coat, four funny white feet, and the white star gleaming on its forehead. 'I once read a book called *Black Beauty*,' he said. 'Couldn't we call your pony that? He's black and he's a real beauty!'

'Oh yes!' cried Lotta. And so Black Beauty was named and became Lotta's, and the little girl could hardly bear to leave him in his stable and go to her dinner.

They all rode home afterwards, talking and laughing. Lou led the horse that Lotta had ridden, and Lotta herself rode on Black Beauty, who now had saddle and bridle and was as meek as before he had been fierce.

The little girl was very proud. This was the first horse she had ever had that was really and truly her own. She meant to train him herself, and her head was full of all kinds of things that she would teach her lovely Black Beauty. She was so happy that she sang aloud, and Jimmy was glad. He thought she looked fine riding the little pony, her hair as black as the pony's shining coat!

They rode into the camp and everyone turned out to see Black Beauty. Mr Galliano praised the pony loudly.

'You have chosen well, Lotta,' he said. 'It is a good beast, yes.'

'This girl is a wonder with horses,' said Lou. 'She should be in the ring, Mr Galliano.'

'Well, her mother and father thought it would be better for her not to go into the ring whilst they were abroad,' said Mrs Brown. 'They thought she might do something too daring if they were not there with her.'

'Oh!' cried Lotta, 'so that's why I wasn't allowed to go into the ring! Oh, it's a shame! Oh, Mr Galliano, please say I may, if I train Black Beauty properly! I will, I will, I will!'

Mr Galliano laughed. 'We will see, yes, we will see,' he said. 'It will not be long now before your parents are back, my little Lotta. Train your pony well, and maybe one day we will see you in the ring!'

Jimmy brought Lucky to make friends with Black Beauty. The little dog liked the pony at once, and Black Beauty dropped his head to sniff at the small creature that stood on its hind legs to reach his nose!

'They're friends already!' cried Jimmy, in delight. 'Oh, Lotta, what an exciting time we're having lately!'

'Yes,' said Lotta, trotting her pony over to the stables to ask Lou where she might put Black Beauty. 'Yes, we *are* having adventures lately, but Black Beauty is the nicest adventure of all! My own horse, my very, very own! I am the luckiest girl in the world—and you are a dear, Jimmy, to buy him for me. I hope he didn't cost too much money.'

'No,' said Jimmy, though the pony had cost him nearly every bit of the money he had saved. But what did that matter? Lucky and he would earn plenty more, and Lotta was happy. Black Beauty would be just as much of a success as Lucky had been—and oh, what fun if they could teach Lucky to do some tricks with Black Beauty!

'We break camp tomorrow!' said Mrs Brown that night to two tired children. 'Up early, both of you!'

'Oooh! Bears at our next camp!' said Jimmy. 'Shan't I like that! Bears, Lotta! Bears, Lucky! What fun we'll have!'

The Bears Join the Circus

Next day the circus was on the move again. Once
more the tents were taken down and Brownie was
very busy. Soon the circus procession was on the
road—cages, caravans, long strings of horses, and
old Jumbo patiently pulling the three largest cages
behind him.

Lotta was not in the caravan this time. Where was
she? She was riding her new pony, Black Beauty,
who was now perfectly obedient! How proud Lotta
was as she rode on her beautiful pony! For once in
a way she had brushed her short hair till it shone,
and had put on her prettiest frock, for she felt that
a lovely thing like Black Beauty deserved a fine
rider!

Little dog Lucky was running about on her hind
legs, but you may be sure that Jimmy was keeping
a sharp eye on her. Since she had been stolen the
little boy had hardly let her out of his sight. Lucky
was already fond of Black Beauty, and for most of
the journey the little dog ran on all fours by

Beauty's heels, or walked on her hind legs by her nose. Sometimes the pony put down his proud little head and lightly touched the clever dog. Then Lucky gave a little yelp and tried to lick Black Beauty's nose!

'Hhrrrrrmph!' suddenly sneezed the elephant. Black Beauty was so startled that she stood straight up on her hind legs like Lucky! Lotta nearly fell off, and Jimmy shouted with laughter.

'You wait till I get you, Jimmy!' cried Lotta.

'It did look funny, Black Beauty and Lucky both up on their hind legs!' said Jimmy. 'I half thought old Jumbo would stand up too!'

They came to their next show-place at last. There was still a day before the circus opened. Mr Galliano was expecting the bears that day, for he wanted to see them perform in the ring before the show opened.

A large travelling-cage was already in the great field when Mr Galliano's people arrived. Jimmy looked at it and gave a shout.

'The bears! It must be the bears! Come and see, Lotta.'

'I must see to Black Beauty first,' said Lotta, and she slipped down from the pony's smooth back. She put her arms around his neck and the pony nuzzled against her. Then the little girl led him off to have

How proud Lotta was as she rode on her beautiful pony!

a feed and a good rub-down. She was simply delighted with her pony. She longed to teach him how to dance, and how to gallop round and round the ring whilst she did tricks on his back.

The bears were in their cage. There were five of them, three not much more than year-old cubs. They were dark brown, fat, and clumsy. Jimmy went to the bars of their cage and spoke to them.

The bears took no notice, but as the little boy went on talking, one of the cubs walked over to him with shambling feet.

'Hi there! Come away!' shouted a voice suddenly. Jimmy turned and saw a fat man running towards him. 'Do you want to get clawed?' shouted the man.

'It's all right, Mr Volla!' said Tonks, who was nearby. 'That's Jimmy, our Boy Wonder! He went into the tigers' cage at our last show, and all they did was to purr at him like cats. Those bears will be eating out of his hand in five minutes!'

'Ah,' said Mr Volla, who had moustaches like Mr Galliano, 'so that's Jimmy. I've heard of him. He's got a marvellous dog, hasn't he?'

'Yes, I have,' said Jimmy proudly. 'There she is, look!'

Lucky trotted up to Mr Volla, and then did the new trick that Jimmy had been teaching her—turning

head-over-heels as fast as ever she could—over—
and over—and over! Mr Volla laughed.

'I've never seen a dog do that before!' he said.
'But my bears can do it, though not so neatly as
Lucky. Hup, bears, hup! Over you go!'

Mr Volla cracked a small whip he had, and all the
bears got up on their hind legs. One by one they
turned head-over-heels, but they did it so comically
that Jimmy laughed till he cried.

'They do it just like Stanley the clown when he
wants to be very funny,' said Jimmy.

'Ah,' said Mr Volla, 'bears are the clowns of the
animal world, you know. They are clumsy, and they
know they're funny. They love it. You must come
and watch them in the ring this afternoon when they
perform for Mr Galliano. Two of them put on
boxing-gloves and pretend to fight. They'll make
you laugh all right!'

So that afternoon Jimmy went to watch the bears.
They were real clowns, there was no doubt about
it—and how they loved to fool about and be funny!
They each had a stool to sit on, and one bear made
it his business to wait behind one or other of the
bears and take away his stool just as he was going
to sit down! Of course the other bear fell flop!

'That cub, Bobby, thought of the trick himself,'
said Mr Volla proudly. 'You don't have to teach him

145

anything! He may look clumsy and slow, but his brain's as good as any clown's!'

The bears all knew their own stools. They could dance slowly and clumsily on their big hind feet, and Dobby and another bear, Susie, took paws and did a sort of clumsy polka together, which sent everyone into fits of laughter.

Then another two bears, Grizel and Tubby, had boxing-gloves put on their enormous paws, and they boxed with one another, getting some smacking blows on their noses and chests. Suddenly Grizel gave Tubby such a loud smack that Tubby sat down with a grunt and wouldn't get up again! Then all the other bears grunted loudly and clapped their paws together so that their great claws clattered.

Then Mr Volla cracked his whip again, and Dobby went to fetch a big football. Dear me, how funny those bears were with that football! They kicked it, they dribbled it, they fell over it, they hugged it! And then, when Mr Volla cracked his whip once again, they all solemnly took paws and danced round to the music of 'Ring-a-ring-of-roses', and when it came to the words, '*All* fall down!' down fell every bear, plop!

Everybody clapped hard. The bears got up and bowed, waving their big, flappy paws and winking their small eyes. They were a great joke.

Jimmy was thrilled. Here were animals that really liked being funny. He loved them. So did Lucky. The little dog sitting beside Jimmy had watched the bears all the time.

'Oh, Mr Galliano, the bears are much better than the tigers!' cried Jimmy. 'Tigers hate doing tricks, and it's a shame to make them. But bears just love being clowns. Look at Dobby pretending to do a dance all by himself!'

So he was. Mr Volla had taken the other bears off, but Dobby had turned back and come to do a little show all by himself in the ring. His eyes twinkled. He loved showing off.

Mr Volla's whip cracked from outside the ring. Dobby dropped down on all fours and shambled off, grunting. Everybody clapped again.

'They are good, yes,' said Mr Galliano. 'You are right, Jimmy. It is better to have animals that love their work. The bears will be a great success, yes!'

And they certainly were! When the circus opened the next night, the audience stood up in their seats and cheered each turn. Sammy the chimpanzee; Jumbo playing cricket; Lilliput's clever monkeys; Oona the acrobat's amazing tricks; Sticky Stanley the clown's comical ways; Jimmy and his dog Lucky; Lou, Pepita, and Juanita and their beautiful dancing horses—they were all cheered and cheered again, but the bears got the biggest cheers of all!

Mr Galliano stood in the ring, dressed in his tight-fitting red coat, his top hat well on one side, and his moustaches very long and curling, as pleased as could be. His whip cracked for every new turn, and only one person in his circus was just a little bit impatient.

That was Lotta. How she longed to go into the ring with her lovely Black Beauty! If only she could hurry up and teach him to dance and to do all the things a circus pony had to learn! Then Lotta could go into the ring too!

Mr Galliano caught sight of Lotta as he strode out of the ring, and saw her longing eyes fixed on the sawdust circle.

'Cheer up!' he said. 'We shall do well here! It will be fine for everybody, yes!'

'Mr Galliano, can I go into the ring too, if I teach Black Beauty?' begged Lotta, 'You did say I could, didn't you?'

'Yes, you may,' said Mr Galliano. 'But we cannot make a new turn for you, Lotta. You will have to ask Lou if you may share a little of his turn.

Lotta was not pleased with this. She knew quite well that circus folk hate sharing their turn with anyone. Lou and his sisters liked her, but even so

148

she did not think they would let her come in with them. They wanted all the cheers and clapping for themselves and their own horses!

Lotta told Jimmy. He nodded his head. 'Yes,' he said, 'Lou and the others are kind enough, but after all it isn't fair to ask them to let you have some of their own turn, Lotta.'

'Well, what can I do, then?' asked the little girl, almost in tears. 'What's the use of having a fine pony like Black Beauty and teaching him tricks if I can't take him into the ring?'

Jimmy thought for a while, and then he jumped up with a shout. 'I know what we'll do!' he said. 'We will teach Lucky to ride Black Beauty, and then you shall bring your pony into the ring when it's *my* turn! I don't mind sharing my turn with you, Lotta—and perhaps you could begin like that. It would be better than nothing.'

Lotta hugged Jimmy for joy. 'You are the kindest boy!' she cried. 'Oh, Jimmy, let's begin teaching Lucky tomorrow! I'm already teaching Black Beauty his tricks, and he learns like lightning!'

Lotta Gets Her Chance!

The two children began teaching Lucky to ride Black Beauty the very next day. Lucky was always eager to learn new tricks, for she was a very clever dog and loved to use her brains.

She knew how to balance herself on the tight-rope, so she found it easy enough to sit on the pony's broad back, but when Black Beauty began to trot, Lucky found it was not so easy!

She slipped and fell to the ground, but she did not hurt herself of course. Before Jimmy could stop Black Beauty and put Lucky on his back again, the little dog gave a leap and jumped up herself!

'Look at that!' said Jimmy. 'Would you believe it, Lotta? She leapt on that trotting pony just as easily as you do! She's holding her balance better this time, look! She doesn't need teaching! She knows what we want her to do and she's doing her best to learn!'

Black Beauty went cantering round and round the ring for Lotta had already taught her to do this at the right pace. Lucky fell off again, and once more jumped up. She found that by sitting on her tail she could keep her balance quite well. Before the morning had ended the little dog could ride the pony as well as Lotta could.

'Marvellous!' said Lotta, patting the happy little dog. 'Do you know, Jimmy, I believe we could teach Lucky to jump through a paper hoop just as I do! Once she has really got her balance on horseback she can do that, I'm sure.'

The two children taught Lucky and Black Beauty together every morning, working patiently. They never worked the animals too long, for Jimmy had long since learnt that little and often was the best way to teach, and he and Lotta always praised their animals and rewarded them.

'You know, Lotta, animals are just like people,' said Jimmy, as he was brushing Lucky one morning, and Lotta was grooming Black Beauty. 'People with brains love to learn anything and they're always trying new things. Stupid people don't want to learn and can't. Animals are the same. The clever ones long to learn, but it's no use teaching the stupid ones anything. I'm glad I was born with brains, aren't you? It must be dull to be stupid.'

'Yes,' said Lotta. 'But it must be worse to be born clever and be too lazy to use your brains. I've known some people like that, Jimmy—and some animals too.'

'Well, stupid or not, I love all animals,' said Jimmy. 'But it's more fun to be with the clever ones! Isn't it, little dog Lucky?'

Lucky licked her master's hand and yelped. She thought Jimmy was the king of the world, and she was happiest when she was trying to do what Jimmy wanted her to.

Lotta and Jimmy had a fine time with the pony and Lucky. The dog and the pony enjoyed being with one another, and worked together beautifully. Soon Lucky learnt how to leap from Black Beauty's back through a paper hoop held by Jimmy, and back on to the pony's back again! The first time she did this, Jimmy and Lotta shouted for joy. They were sure that when Mr Galliano saw the trick he would let Lotta bring her pony into the ring at last.

Lotta worked hard with Black Beauty too, teaching him to waltz as the other horses did. The little girl brought the gramophone from the caravan and Jimmy wound it up and put the records on for Black Beauty to waltz to.

Black Beauty, unlike most of the dancing horses, had a perfect sense of time. He danced slowly if the record played slowly, and quickly if it played quickly. He was very nimble on his feet, and loved the music.

He let Lotta do anything she liked with him. She had been the first to conquer him and he loved the little girl with his wild little heart, though he would not let anyone else touch him except Mr Galliano and Jimmy.

Lotta rode him at full speed, and then, at a shout, he would stop dead! The little girl would be thrown right over his head, but she knew how to fall and, like a cat, always landed on her feet! Black Beauty would then gallop full speed round the ring again, and Lotta would wait till he came by and leap up safely on his back.

She could ride him kneeling on one or both knees. She could ride him standing forwards or backwards. She could jump through a paper hoop held by Jimmy, and she could do something else very difficult too. This was a trick her father could do.

The trick was to lower herself under the pony's body and come up the other side safely, to sit on his back, whilst he was cantering round the ring! It was a dangerous trick, for if she slipped and fell, the pony's hoofs might cut her—but Lotta was not even afraid of that! She felt sure that Black Beauty would be clever enough not to tread on her.

She never did fall, because she was very nimble, and soon learnt to swing herself under Black Beauty's middle and up the other side. Lucky ran alongside, yelping excitedly, and sometimes Lotta would lean right down and pick Lucky up. Then they would stand up on the pony together, Lotta yelling and Lucky barking like mad.

The children always chose the early morning for their practice, because they did not want anyone else to guess what they were doing. And also, others needed the ring for practising in later on in the day. Circus folk do not need just to know their tricks— they must practise always, all the time.

At last Jimmy felt that little dog Lucky had learnt his horseback tricks perfectly, so he went to speak to Mr Galliano.

'Lucky can ride on Black Beauty, sir, and jump through the hoops,' said the little boy. 'If you would come and watch one morning, perhaps you'd like the new turn and say we could do it one night.'

So Mr Galliano came to watch, and his eyes nearly fell out of his head when he saw Lucky's new tricks.

'That dog is human, yes!' he said. 'You will teach him to dress as a ring-master, wear a top hat, and crack a whip next! Yes! Bring Black Beauty into the ring tonight, and Lucky shall do his new trick.'

'May Lotta bring her pony into the ring, please, Mr Galliano?' said Jimmy. 'She has helped me to teach Lucky, you know, and it's her pony.'

'Very well, she may do that,' said Mr Galliano. 'Tell her to wear her circus frock.'

Jimmy flew off to tell Lotta the good news. She was to go into the ring again! Oh, what fun!

'And, Lotta, you must ride round the ring once or twice yourself, and stand up on Black Beauty, just to get a few claps!' said Jimmy. 'Maybe if the people like you, Mr Galliano will let you do more another night. Get your circus frock out and we'll see if it's clean.'

It was clean—but alas it no longer fitted Lotta, who had grown very much the last few months. The little girl was ready to cry. She knew she could not go into the ring unless she had a proper frock.

'Now, don't be a baby!' said Mrs Brown, putting on her hat and taking up her basket. 'Come along into the town with me, and we'll buy what we need for you. I can run it up with my sewing machine in no time and make you look a real little fairy!'

'Oh, Mrs Brown, you're a darling!' cried Lotta, and she put on her shoes and rushed after Mrs Brown.

Well, what a busy time Lotta, Mrs Galliano and Mrs Brown had that day, making a new frock for Lotta. They had bought gauzy stuff set with shining silver spangles, and they made the little girl a fluffy dress of this, that stood out in a short skirt like a fairy's frock. The little bodice had silver spangles on too.

Her old silver crown and wand she could use again, but new silvery stockings had to be bought.

155

Her long silver wings were mended and repainted with silver paint—and then everything was ready, down to the silver shoes that had been bought with the stockings. They had no heels and were well-rubbed with resin so that Lotta would not slip when standing on her pony.

And now it was nearly time for the show to begin! People were already crowding in at the gate, for Mr Galliano's circus was famous. The lights were flaring in the 'big top', as the circus folk called their show tent, and Lotta was almost beside herself with excitement.

At last it was Jimmy's turn with Lucky. What a shout went up as the little boy ran into the ring, bowing to everyone, with Lucky at his heels. Jimmy looked fine in his glittering suit with its short red cloak—like a little prince, Lotta thought.

Lucky went all through her marvellous tricks, and when at last Jimmy cried, 'Spell me the name of the man who has the finest circus!' and Lucky fetched out eight letters from the pile and arranged them to spell 'Galliano', the people clapped till their hands hurt them!

This was usually Lucky's last trick—but tonight there was more to come. Lotta suddenly rode in on Black Beauty! The people stared in astonishment. Many of them had been to Galliano's circus before and they had not seen this trick.

The little girl looked lovely in her silver fairy-frock. She jumped off Black Beauty and led her to Jimmy.

'Up then, up!' cried Jimmy to Lucky, and up the little dog jumped! Off went the pony, and Lucky rode on his back in delight. Down he came when Jimmy called, and then up again whilst the pony was galloping. Everybody cheered. The dog was even cleverer than they had thought!

Lotta held out a paper hoop. Lucky jumped through it and landed back safely on Black Beauty. Again she jumped through another hoop. She had been so perfectly trained that she knew exactly what to do.

That was enough for the first night. Mr Galliano came into the ring to crack his whip and end the turn. Jimmy and Lucky bowed and ran out. Lotta was about to follow on Black Beauty, when somebody got up and shouted:

'Let's see the little girl have a turn! Up you go, Missie, and let's see what you can do!'

Everybody shouted and clapped. They wanted to see Lotta, too, do something, for they felt sure she could. Lotta did not dare to ride round, for she had heard Mr Galliano's whip crack and knew she must go. Mr Galliano stood wondering what to do. It was Oona's turn next. Should he give Lotta a chance, though?

'Go on, Missie,' yelled the people. Mr Galliano turned and nodded to Lotta, who was trembling with excitement.

'Get up and do what you can,' he said. And Lotta jumped on to Black Beauty's back. At last she had got her chance—at last, at last, at last!

Good Luck for the Children

Lotta knew that Black Beauty felt her excitement too. The pony was longing to show what he could do. He was a real circus animal, and loved the smell of the sawdust and the flaring lights.

Mr Galliano cracked his whip again. Lotta made a sign for music. The band struck up a merry tune, and Black Beauty pricked up his ears. Like most horses, he loved music and would not have minded practising all day long if only he had had tunes played to him!

'Round you go!' said Lotta in his ear, and the pony began to dance round and round, his hoofs keeping perfect time to the music.

The bandsmen were astonished. They were used to making the time of their music follow the dancing of the horses, but this pony followed the time of their music as if he could hear the beats properly!

So the band played in perfect time, and Black Beauty danced round and round, lifting his hoofs daintily and tossing his lovely head with its white star. The watching people thought him beautiful, but only the circus folk knew how clever it was for a horse to keep such good time with the music.

The music stopped. The drummer rolled loudly on his drum—the signal for Lotta to gallop him round and round and begin any trick she knew.

She called to Black Beauty, and he at once galloped at top speed round the ring, his hoofs making a muffled clatter on the sawdust. Lotta gave a yell, and Black Beauty stopped at once, as he had been taught. Lotta flew over his head, turned a half-somersault, and landed neatly on her feet.

But everyone had thought that she was going to be thrown and hurt, and they shouted. Even Mr Galliano was startled, but when he saw the neat way in which Lotta landed on her feet like a falling cat, he knew it was a clever trick.

The pony went galloping round the ring by himself. Lotta waited till he came round again and then deftly leapt up on to his back once more. At her next yell the pony stopped again, and once more Lotta went hurtling over his head, to fall on her feet. This time the people knew what she was doing, and they clapped loudly.

Lotta jumped back on to Black Beauty. She was enjoying herself, and so was the pony. How glad the

Lotta jumped back on to Black Beauty.

little girl was that she had practised so hard each morning!

She knelt up on the pony's back. She stood up, a graceful little figure, bumping up and down with the pony, her long silver wings outspread, and her silvery dress glittering like moonlight. Jimmy thought she looked lovely—and what a clever, daring little girl she was!

Lotta stood on one foot and waved the other in the air! Then she lightly leapt round and faced the back of the horse. She stood on one foot again and waved to the people, whilst all the time black Beauty galloped solemnly round the ring.

Mr Galliano was astonished to find how well Lotta had trained her pony in such a short time. But he was even more astonished at Lotta's next trick of slipping right underneath Black Beauty and coming up the other side of him!

'Too dangerous, yes, too dangerous!' muttered Mr Galliano to himself. There wasn't a sound as the little girl did this daring trick; but goodness, how everyone clapped and cheered when they saw Lotta sitting safely up on the pony once more, waving cheekily to them!

Lucky suddenly came bounding into the ring. He wanted to do a trick with Lotta too! The little girl, who was about to bow and gallop off, gave a shout.

She galloped near Lucky, swung right down from the pony, and picked up the little dog! She set him on the seat in front of her. Then she stood up again on the galloping pony and shouted to Lucky. 'Up then, up!'

And Lucky stood up too! So there they were, the two of them, standing cleverly on the pony as it raced round the ring! Jimmy ran into the ring to watch.

Mr Galliano's whip cracked. Lotta must gallop out. So out she went through the thick red curtains, waving her hand and smiling, the prettiest little figure that anyone could wish to see!

The people stood up and cheered her. They had not expected to see this. She had been one of the successes of the evening, one of the best things in a very good show.

The little girl was almost crying with joy when she leapt off Black Beauty. She could hear the people still clapping and cheering, and she knew she had been a success.

'Oh, Jimmy, Black Beauty was wonderful tonight!' she cried. 'He did everything perfectly. He's the finest pony I have ever known.'

'And you are the best little circus rider I have ever seen!' cried Mr Wally, as he passed with Sammy the chimpanzee. 'A splendid show, Lotta! You must have practised very hard indeed.'

'She did,' said Jimmy proudly. 'She practises every single morning.'

Then up came Lou, Pepita, and Juanita, full of admiration and praise for Lotta and Black Beauty. They were not at all jealous of the little girl's success, for they were kindly folk, and Lotta had been a great help to them in looking after their string of beautiful white horses.

After the show was over, Mr Galliano sent for Jimmy and Lotta, but this time they went gladly, for they knew they had not been fetched to be scolded.

'You are not afraid to come and see me this time—no?' said Mr Galliano, smiling his big smile at them both, his top hat almost over one ear. 'You are good, hard-working children, yes! You, Lotta, may go into the ring with Jimmy each night, and work up a turn together. It is better that you two children should be together in the show. You shall be the two Wonder Children, yes!'

'Thank you, Mr Galliano!' they said, both together, their hearts full of joy. To do a turn together! This was even better than they had hoped. What fun they would have with Lucky and Beauty in the ring! What tricks they would teach that lively, clever pair!

Already Jimmy was seeing Lucky dressed like Mr Galliano, in riding breeches, red coat, top hat, and whip, riding on Black Beauty! And Lotta, too, was making pictures in her mind of all the things the four would do together!

'Won't Lal and Laddo be pleased when they come back and find I'm in the ring too!' cried Lotta, when she got back to the Browns' caravan and told Jimmy's father and mother all about everything.

'I hope they will,' said Mrs Brown, ladling out hot soup, which the children always had after the show at night. 'You know, they said they didn't much want Lotta to go into the ring whilst they were away, as they thought the rest would do her good, and she could learn her lessons better and be taught how to be neat and clean.'

'Oh, Mrs Brown! I *have* learnt my lessons well, and I really have tried to be neat and clean!' cried Lotta. 'I know how to read and write now, and I can do quite hard sums! And now my hair is short, I'm sure I look as tidy as Jimmy!'

Mrs Brown looked at Lotta's head with its close curling mop of hair and laughed. 'You've been a very good little girl,' she said, 'and you deserve all this. Now the next thing to look forward to is your father and mother coming home. They will soon be back in the circus.'

'It will be lovely to have them again,' said Lotta. 'But oh, I shall miss living here in your nice caravan with you and Brownie and Jimmy and Lucky and Lulu, Mrs Brown.'

'Well, you must just see that you keep your own caravan pretty and nice,' said Mrs Brown. 'And you know that you can come here to us whenever you like—your little bed will always be ready for you.'

Lotta got up and gave Mrs Brown a hug. She felt so happy that night that she could have hugged anyone, even the bears!

The two children got into their bunks at last, but they couldn't go to sleep. They talked and talked about the happenings of the show that night till Mrs Brown could bear it no longer. She was tired herself and wanted to go to sleep.

'Another word from either of you and I shall get out and give you each a good scolding!' she said. Not another sound was heard from either of them!

Things Go Wrong

And now, each night, Lotta and Jimmy went into the ring together, with little dog Lucky and Black Beauty the pony. The people loved to see the beautiful pony, with his four white feet and his brilliant white star on his forehead. They loved Lucky too, and Mr Galliano was pleased to see what a great success the two children were, with their well-trained animals.

The circus stayed for some time and then, as it always did, packed up and went on the road once more. It was full summer now, and the countryside was beautiful. Poppies nodded along the wayside, and Lotta picked a bunch, weaved them into a garland, and hung it round Beauty's black shining neck.

When the circus procession went through the towns now, Lotta, dressed in her shining circus frock, rode proudly on Black Beauty, and waved to the astonished children that lined the roadside to watch her pass. Sometimes Lucky rode with her, and he too waved a cheeky paw, much to everyone's delight.

And once even Jemima came to ride with Lotta and Lucky, and such a crowd came to see that a policeman had to come and push the people away so that the procession could go on! Really, it was all great fun, and the children enjoyed themselves tremendously.

One day Lotta had a letter from her mother. She could not read handwriting very well, although she could now read books, so she gave it to Jimmy to read to her.

'DEAR LOTTA' (said the letter), 'we hope to meet you at the next show place. We have written to Mr Galliano. I hope you have been a good girl. We have not had any letters from you for some time, so we do not know how you are getting on. You will soon have to start practising again, so that you may join us in the ring. We have some fine new horses.— Love from

LAL.'

Lotta was pleased with her mother's letter. 'Oh, Jimmy!' she said, dancing about and making Lucky dance about too. 'Oh, Jimmy! My mother doesn't know that I go into the ring every night! Won't she be surprised! Oh, isn't it lovely, I shall see Lal and Laddo at our next show place!'

The children looked out for Lal and Laddo at the next show place, but they had not yet arrived in the camp. Lotta was longing to show her mother and father her lovely Black Beauty. The camp settled in as usual, and once more the 'big top' went up, and the caravans and cages took up their places in the field.

The next day two great travelling horse-boxes drew up outside the field and began to try to get in through the wide gate. On the sides of the vans were painted in large red letters, 'Lal and Laddo's Wonder Horses'. Lotta gave such a scream of delight that Mrs Brown dropped the spoon into the stew she was stirring.

'It's Lal and Laddo!' she shouted. 'Oh, it's my father and mother back again!'

She flew like the wind to the field-gate and looked anxiously for Lal and Laddo. She saw Laddo at once, and rushed to him. She leapt into his strong arms, and he hugged and kissed his little daughter, delighted to see her looking so well and happy.

'My, how you've grown!' he said. 'We've missed you, Lotta.'

'Where's my mother—where's Lal? cried Lotta. Laddo's face grew sad. 'She's ill,' he said. 'She was

taken ill yesterday on the way here, and I have had
to leave her in hospital. But she will be better in a
month or two, Lotta, so don't worry. She had a fall
while we were away, and hurt her back. She would
not rest it properly, and now it is very bad again, and
the doctor says she must stay in bed for five or six
weeks.'

Lotta's face crumpled up and she began to cry.
She had so much looked forward to her mother
coming back again.

'We'll go and see her tomorrow,' promised Laddo.
'Don't fret, Lotta.'

The little girl blinked back her tears. She was
dreadfully disappointed. She had looked forward so
much to showing her mother her lovely new pony,
and to seeing her face when she saw Lotta in the
ring. And now she wouldn't be able to show her
Black Beauty for ages and ages!

'Why can't Lal come to the camp and rest in our
own caravan instead of in a faraway hospital?' she
asked. 'I can look after her! I can do everything
nicely now. Mrs Brown has taught me.'

'Well, Lotta,' said Laddo, 'I'm afraid I won't be
able to join this circus now Lal is away. I must work
with a partner, you know, and the only one I can get
in Lal's place is Madame Fifinella and she belongs
to another circus. I'm afraid I will have to go there.

I just came here to see you and to tell you the news. I must see Mr Galliano too. Perhaps he can keep on Lou and his sisters.'

Lotta walked into the field with Laddo. The little girl was too horrified even to cry. Everything was going wrong—just when things had seemed so lovely too!

She hadn't got her mother, and wouldn't have her for weeks. Now even her father, Laddo, was going away to another circus. Would she have to go with him? Another circus would not allow her to have a turn all to herself. And how could she possibly bear to leave Jimmy and Lucky?

But she knew her father would want her, for he loved her and would not wish to leave her behind, now that he had come home again. She left him to go and see Mr Galliano, and then she ran behind the Browns' caravan, sat on an upturned pail, and let the tears run down her cheeks.

Lulu the spaniel came up and licked the tears as they fell. Lotta suddenly felt as if she wanted Black Beauty to comfort her and not Lulu. She ran to the stable where he stood, and he turned his lovely head towards his little mistress. At once he knew she was unhappy and he put his long nose on to her shoulder, whinnying gently.

Jimmy found them there when he went into the stable and he stood still in astonishment. 'Lotta! Whatever's the matter?'

Lotta told him everything, between her tears, and the little boy looked more dismayed than Lotta had ever seen him. Lose Lotta! Lose Black Beauty! Not have Lal and Laddo back after all! This was dreadful.

He sat down on a tub, feeling his legs suddenly weak. Lotta wiped her eyes and looked at him. 'Can't you think of *anything* that would make things better?' she asked him in despair.

Suddenly an idea came into Jimmy's mind. He jumped up and took Lotta's hand. 'Lotta!' he said. 'I know! *I* know! Why shouldn't you be Laddo's partner? He doesn't know how well you've been doing in the ring! He doesn't know you've got a pony of your own! He can train you to do anything he wants done in a very short while, because you have been practising so well lately.'

'Oh, Jimmy,' cried Lotta, her eyes shining like stars at once. 'Do you really suppose he'd let me? I am sure I can do everything that Madame Fifinella can! And I don't mind how hard I have to work! But what about Lal, my mother?'

'Well, you silly, if you and Laddo are working together in our circus, you can have Lal back in your

172

'Lotta! Whatever's the matter?'

own caravan and look after her till she's better!'
cried Jimmy. 'You say she only wants a good rest—
well, she'll be much happier here with us, seeing
you do well in the ring, than away by herself in a
strange place!'

'Jimmy—oh, Jimmy, I believe you've thought of
the very idea!' cried Lotta.

'Let's come and tell Mr Galliano this very
minute!' said Jimmy. 'Quick, before he fixes up for
Lou and Pepita and Juanita to stay on! Let's hope
Laddo hasn't already fixed up with Madame
Fifinella!'

Black Beauty whinnied gently. He was pleased to
hear a happier sound in Lotta's voice. The little girl
jumped on his back and cantered out into the open,
her face still tear-stained but her eyes eager and
bright. Jimmy followed her, with Lucky and Lulu
at his heels.

They went to Mr Galliano's caravan. Inside they
could hear Galliano's deep voice and Laddo's
strong one, and they could hear the clatter of teacups
as Mrs Galliano washed up.

Jimmy rapped on the open door.

'I am busy, yes,' called Mr Galliano. 'Go away for
a little while.'

'But please, Mr Galliano, we must see you now!'
called Jimmy, 'Please let us come up.'

Mr Galliano made an impatient noise. He was not in a good temper, for he was very disappointed to hear Laddo's news. 'Come, then,' he said. 'What is it you children want?'

Goodbye—and Good Luck!

Jimmy and Lotta ran up the caravan steps. Mr Galliano glared at them.

'Why do you come disturbing me now?' he said. 'You see I am busy—yes?'

'I'm very sorry, Mr Galliano,' said Jimmy, 'but we've had such a good idea, Lotta and I. Please, sir, why can't Lotta be Laddo's partner, instead of getting Madame Fifinella and going away to another circus? She's as good as any grown-up circus rider—I heard you say so yourself to Mr Tonks the other day.'

'Your ears are too long,' grumbled Mr Galliano. Laddo looked up, astonished.

'Has Lotta been in the ring by herself then?' he asked. 'You have not heard that—no?' said Galliano. 'Ah, she is certainly a wonder, that little Lotta, though she still has much to learn. Yes, Laddo, she now has a pony of her own, the cleverest animal I have seen for years. And she and that pony perform each night in the ring with Jimmy and Lucky. It is a very good turn, yes.'

'She has worked and practised so hard, Laddo,' said Jimmy earnestly. 'She could really do all you needed if only you'd teach her what she doesn't know. She has watched Juanita and Pepita too, and she can do nearly all they can do. Couldn't you let her try for a few weeks, and then perhaps Lal will be ready to take her place again?'

'That is for Mr Galliano to say,' said Laddo, still looking very astonished to think that his small daughter had been working so hard and doing such surprising things.

Mr Galliano drummed his fingers on the table. He turned to Mrs Galliano, who was still washing up, and listening.

'What do you think, Tessa?' he said. 'Will Lotta do for a few weeks?'

Mrs Galliano was fond of the two children, and she looked at Lotta. 'She would do, I think,' she said. 'It would be too much to give her such hard work for very long, but for a few weeks, yes, it would not matter. She is a clever little girl and not afraid of hard work.'

Mr Galliano always thought a lot of his wife's words. She did not talk much, but what she said was always sensible. He slapped his hand on the table and made everyone jump.

'It is settled then!' he said. 'Lotta becomes your little partner for a few weeks till Lal is well again— and you will write to tell Fifinella you do not need her after all—yes?'

'Yes, Mr Galliano,' said Laddo, surprised and delighted. 'Well, then, sir, Lal could come back to our caravan, couldn't she—and we could look after her ourselves. She would be so much happier and would get better so much more quickly if she were with the people she knows and loves.'

'Certainly, certainly, certainly!' said Mr Galliano. 'Fetch her tomorrow, yes. Tessa, things look better. We will all have strawberry ice-cream for dinner!'

That was always Mr Galliano's way. When he was pleased he would send ice-creams or bottles of ginger beer, or whatever came into his head, to all his circus folk. He had a hot temper but a very kind heart, and all his people thought the world of him. He pushed his top hat well on one side and nodded goodbye to Laddo and the children.

Lotta and Jimmy were overjoyed. Lotta ran squealing with delight to Mrs Brown's caravan, and for the second time that morning Mrs Brown dropped the spoon into the stew. 'Lotta! I won't have you …' she began.

But Lotta didn't let her finish. She caught hold of Mrs Brown by the waist and danced round the caravan with her, shouting at the top of her voice:

'Lal's coming back tomorrow! I'm going to be Laddo's partner! He's not leaving the circus!'

Mrs Brown, who had known nothing of what had happened, was quite bewildered. She pushed Lotta away and sat down, out of breath.

'Now, Lotta, behave!' she said. 'Tell me things from the beginning, you silly child. I've no idea what you are talking about.'

So Jimmy and Lotta, both talking at once, told the news. Lucky barked with excitement and Lulu whined. It was difficult to understand anything, but Mrs Brown listened patiently. In the middle of the story, Black Beauty, who had been left outside, became impatient, walked up the steps and stuck his head inside the caravan!

'Well, I never!' said Mrs Brown. 'There's that pony of yours in the caravan now, Lotta. Well, I've had dogs and monkeys, but I won't have horses. Shoo, shoo, Beauty!'

So Beauty shooed, and stood outside, whinnying for Lotta. Mrs Brown heard the rest of the story and was pleased.

'I'm glad we can have Lal back,' she said. 'Well, Lotta, you and I will be busy getting your caravan clean and tidy today, ready for Lal tomorrow, if she's coming. Jimmy, I shall have a list of shopping for you to do, for Lotta's larder will want stocking. You'd better have your dinners straight away, and then we can start.'

Dinner was lovely, for the pudding was strawberry ice-cream, of course, and really it was surprising how much those two children could eat!

Laddo's horses were now safely in the circus field. Lou and his sisters were packing up, for they were going to join another circus, after having a well-earned holiday. The children were sorry to say goodbye to them, for they were fond of the three riders and of their lovely white horses. But circus life is made up of 'Hellos' and 'Goodbyes', and the children were used to it.

Lotta and Mrs Brown spent very happy, busy hours getting ready Lal's caravan. The little girl hummed as she scrubbed the floor. Lulu wondered why she was so happy and kept coming up to lick her. Lotta had to keep pushing her down the caravan steps because her paws dirtied the nice clean floor!

The mats were beaten well. Jimmy cleaned the windows. Mrs Brown sent him down to the town for some new blue cotton, and quickly made some pretty curtains herself for the windows.

The stove, which had not been used for months, was cleaned so that it shone. The little larder was washed from top to bottom, and as soon as the shelves were dry Jimmy put clean paper on each one.

'Goodness!' said Lotta, in surprise. 'Lal won't know her larder all dressed up in paper-lined shelves. We've never done that before.'

'Well, it's time you began then,' said Mrs Brown, briskly. 'You know enough now, Lotta, to be able to keep your caravan beautifully, and just see that you do, or I'll be after you with a broom!'

Lotta laughed in delight. 'You can come after me with six brooms!' she said. 'But you wouldn't catch me!'

Then off she went with Jimmy to buy all the things for her mother's larder. She skipped along very happily, and Jimmy was glad too. What a good thing he had given Lotta her lovely Black Beauty, and how lucky it was that the little girl had worked so hard!

Laddo set off to fetch Lal from the hospital. He had hired a car and put plenty of soft cushions at the back. Lotta wanted to come with him but he said no, he wanted Lal to be quite quiet in the car, and she would get too excited if Lotta were there, telling her all the news.

So the two children waited in patience—or rather, in *im*patience, for they hopped up and down, ran into the road to see if the car was coming back, hopped up and down again, chased each other, and were altogether quite mad!

Then at last the car came back and the two children set up such a yell! Everyone came running up, for all the circus folk wanted to welcome back Lal, whom they loved. The car drove slowly in at the field-gate, Laddo trying not to bump over the ruts. Lal waved to everyone from the back.

'Welcome home, Lal, welcome home!' yelled everyone. 'Hurrah! Hurrah!'

How glad Lal was to come back to the circus she knew and loved so well! Laddo carried her carefully into the pretty caravan and Mrs Brown tucked her into bed. Lotta was wild with delight to have her mother back again. She hugged her at least twenty times, and told her proudly all that she was going to do. Black Beauty was allowed to come up the steps of Laddo's caravan to be seen by Lal and admired.

'He is the best pony you could have chosen,' said Lal, stroking his soft nose. Lal could stroke and fondle any horse, however wild, for like Lotta, she had a way with horses. 'He is clever, independent, and loyal. You are a lucky girl, Lotta.'

'She deserves it all, though,' said Jimmy. 'She really has worked hard, Lal, and every day she has helped Lou and the others, though she knew she could not go into the ring with them. I am sure she will be a great success with Laddo till you are better again.'

The day passed quickly, and the night came; the circus was due to open once more. People began to stream in at the gates. The lights flared in the 'big top', and Oona strewed fresh sawdust over the ring.

We will leave Jimmy and Lotta whilst they are so happy. It would be fun to follow them on their way, but all stories have to end. Soon the circus will begin

How they love Jimmy, and what fun they are going to have with him.

once more, and shouts and laughter and the cracking of Mr Galliano's huge whip will fill the great tent.

Oona has finished spreading the sawdust. He has gone to change into his glittering circus suit. Sticky Stanley the clown is already in his suit, and is painting his face a strange mixture of red and white.

Mr Wally is with Sammy the chimpanzee, dressing him in a new coat, talking to his beloved pet as if he were a child. Mr Tonks is rubbing down Jumbo, and he has to climb a ladder to do that! He too is talking to his elephant as if Jumbo were his best friend—and, indeed, he is!

Lilliput is dressing his four monkeys ready for their nightly tea party in the ring. He is scolding Jemima because she has put four hats on, one after the other so that Lilliput could not imagine where they were when he looked for them to put on his monkeys' heads.

Laddo and Lotta are with their horses, giving them a last rub-down to make them shine for the ring. Lotta is very happy. She has on her beautiful frock and looks like a silvery fairy as she trots to and fro. Each time she passes Black Beauty she whispers in his ear, and he whinnies gently, nuzzling after her as she goes.

And Jimmy is—well, where is Jimmy? Not in his caravan, for only Mrs Brown is there, stirring another of her lovely stews. Brownie is busy some-where, as he always is. Jimmy is not with him. He is not with Lotta either, nor is he in the ring, for that is empty, waiting for the first tan-tan-tara of the trumpets and the crack of Galliano's whip.

We must find him and say goodbye to him. He is not with Lilliput. Mr Tonks hasn't seen him. Mr Wally doesn't know where he is.

What is that noise over there in the bears' cage? It sounded like Jimmy laughing!

It *is* Jimmy, and he is playing with the five bears as if he were a bear himself! Mr Galliano has said he may, and Mr Volla is only too pleased to have someone who will make his bears so happy. Lucky is dancing round, barking in glee.

Jimmy is fighting one of the bears with a pair of boxing-gloves on! Smack! Thud! Biff! What a game! All the bears watch and bang their paws on the ground and grunt with joy. How they love Jimmy, and what fun they are going to have with him!

Goodbye, Jimmy! Have a good time. Goodbye, Lucky, little dog Lucky! Maybe we'll see you again some other day!

The End

Other titles in this series:

The Magic Faraway Tree
Folk of the Faraway Tree
Adventures of the Wishing Chair
The Wishing Chair Again
The Enchanted Wood
Naughty Amelia Jane
Amelia Jane Again
More About Amelia Jane
The Book of Fairies
The Book of Brownies
Tales of Toyland & Other Stories
Mr Galliano's Circus
Billy-Bob Tales
The Children of Cherry-Tree Farm
The Children of Willow Farm
More Adventures on Willow Farm
The Adventures of Pip
Tales of Betsy May
Come to the Circus
Hurrah For The Circus
Circus Days Again
The Brer Rabbit Book
Brer Rabbit's a Rascal
Short Story Collection